EXIT STAGE LEFT

WILLIAM PASNAK

SCHOLASTIC INC.
New York Toronto London Auckland Sydney

0-590-41478-X

Cover Design: Dreadnaught

Cover Photograph: Frank Grant

James Lorimer & Company, Publishers
Egerton Ryerson Memorial Building
35 Britain St.,
Toronto, Ontario
M5A 1R7

Exit Stage Left is an original novel based on the **DEGRASSI JUNIOR HIGH** film series, created by Linda Schuyler and Kit Hood. The film series is produced by **PLAYING WITH TIME INC.** with Taylor Productions Inc. and story-edited by Yan Moore.

CHAPTER 1

LD jammed her garage cap over her untidy hair and pinned it there with her ear muffs. Then, in one motion, she shrugged into her coat, grabbed her knapsack, a half-full bag of Ramirez-brand taco chips (*Super Crunchy! Spicy Hot!*) and a piece of leftover Christmas cake, and swung through the door into the garage. As always, she had no time to get to school, and she was in a hurry. If she really motored, she could just make it. It wasn't that she was so fond of school, of course, but she had lately tried to reduce the wear and tear on her father, and being late the first day back from Christmas holidays wouldn't exactly cool him out.

She came to an abrupt halt, though, when she saw her father talking on the battered black wall phone. He was wearing a suit instead of work clothes. The suit looked new.

Since Frank Delacorte had been in hospital with angina a few months earlier, LD had been watching for small differences like this. Small differences might be big warnings, and she could not shake the uneasy feeling that at any moment disaster might fall. She had already lost one parent — her mother had died when she was little. She didn't want to lose her father, too.

" . . . should talk to you about it right away," he was saying. "Would this morning be all right?"

LD felt the small hairs rise along the back of her neck. He was making an appointment! The only appointments her father ever had outside the garage were with doctors.

She wanted to listen to the rest of his conversation, but when he saw her standing in the garage, he twisted his wrist over to show her the time and semaphored "get going" with his eyebrows.

Reluctantly, LD pulled open the door and stepped out onto the icy concrete. As she cut past the pumps, she had to swing wide to avoid a dented Plymouth coming in for gas. The Plymouth was knocking heavily. "Timing," she thought instinctively. "Check the timing."

But she couldn't keep her mind on cars — or school — or anything. With her father's new suit vivid in her mind, LD made the walk to school on automatic pilot. When she got there, the taco chips still rustled untouched in one pocket, and the cake was a damp, shapeless lump in the other.

If LD had been less absorbed in her own thoughts, she would have seen the slim figure of Stephanie Kay trudging down the street a block ahead. It was a frigid morning, with low, iron-gray clouds. An occasional flake of snow went driving by on the breath of a bitter north-east wind. Around her, the city seemed to groan with the cold. Stephanie thought the weather matched her mood perfectly.

"Hi, Steph!" Lucy swung into step with her just as they came in sight of the dark red bulk of Degrassi Junior High. "Did you have a good Christmas?" Lucy's pink ski jacket seemed to glow with a light of its own this morning, and set off her fine, dark features. Looking at her, Stephanie felt herself no longer blonde, but pale and colorless.

"Oh, yeah, great," Steph said without enthusiasm. "How about you?"

"Wonderful!" Lucy said. "My mom and dad were both home for three whole days! We were even going to go skiing, but then my mom had to go into the office. But I got some neat clothes. What did you get?"

"Uh . . . tapes and stuff."

"Great. We'll have to swap some time. My dad brought me the latest Babylon Rubble album from New York. They're so cool — absolutely dynamic. I mean, it really *throbs*."

"Can't wait," said Stephanie. By now they were inside the school, where the air was not only warm, but thick with the clatter of lockers and the babble of students making up for time lost during the Chrismas break.

Lucy peeled off and headed for her locker. "See you in class!"

"Sure thing," Steph said, and banked in the other direction, into the girls' washroom. She came to rest in front of the first sink, her blue shoulder bag in its usual place before her. But instead of diving into the bag and beginning her accustomed transformation, she just stared at herself in the mirror.

Stephanie found herself unbearably plain today, and there was no help to be found in her bag. It contained only books and gym clothes. No make-up, no earrings, no off-the-shoulder tops and skin-tight jeans — none of the add-on magic she had used every morning of last term to make herself over into a "mature" grade eight student. Today was not only the start of a new term; it was the start of a brand new Stephanie. She wasn't sure she could stand it.

The intercom coughed to life. "Good morning, students. Please note that, for scheduling purposes, this Monday will be a Tuesday, although in the cafeteria, it will be a second

Wednesday. Section one cheerleaders will meet on stage in the auditorium at noon — be sure to bring your pom-poms ... " Stephanie tuned the intercom into the background, and found her hands rummaging about, trying to find her usual props and tools. Old habits, it seemed, died hard. She sighed and picked up her bag. Becoming someone new wasn't going to be easy ...

As Stephanie headed from the washroom toward class wearing a simple long-sleeved shirt, scarf and calf-length skirt, she was observed from a distance by Joey Jeremiah. Joey was, by his own admission, the class leader in wit, fashion and intelligence, not to mention general trendiness. Today, for example, he was making a fashion statement by wearing his favorite straw hat and bright green and white palm-tree shirt, with dark glasses hung on the outside of the pocket.

Joey's sharp eyes were the first to note the change in Stephanie. Being a veteran Stephanie-watcher, he knew it was the first time in grade eight she had gone to class wearing the clothes she left home in. He wasn't sure what to make of it, but then he wasn't sure about his feelings for Stephanie anymore, either. He still smarted from her attempt to use him at the end of last term to provoke jealousy, and some action, from his friend Wheels. Coming to school this morning, he had fortified himself to resist her usual glitter and show. He was going to play the field from now on. If Stephanie showed some interest in him, well, he might respond. But for now he wanted to look around. At Lucy, for example, whose parents let her throw parties when they weren't even there. Now someone like that would make a number one, high-status girlfriend . . .

The twins, Erica and Heather, dove upon Stephanie the moment they saw her.

"What's happened?"

"You haven't changed!"

"Is this how you're coming to class?"

"You're not even wearing any make-up!"

This is it, Stephanie thought with a sinking feeling, but she feigned nonchalance. "Oh," she said, "I've grown out of that phase. All that glitz is for little girls. I'm just too mature for that."

"Really? I think you look younger like this," Erica said with brutal frankness.

"Did your mom find out?" asked Heather.

Stephanie was stung. "Thanks a whole lot. For your information, this was a completely personal decision, and I think it's a lot more mature than trying to goop yourself up like some zapped-out TV hostess!"

"Okay, okay," Heather said. "Take it easy."

"Yeah, we didn't mean anything," Erica said. "It's just that you look so . . . different."

"Does anyone else know?"

"Not really," said Stephanie. "I just got here. But I'm sort of dreading seeing everyone."

"It'll be all right," Erica said. "If anyone says anything, we'll tell them you're in mourning."

"You're supposed to wear black for that," Heather pointed out.

"We'll say it was a distant relative. Or the letter carrier."

"Oh, yeah," said Stephanie. "Thanks. That will really help. People will think I'm *really* weird, then."

"Hey," said Erica, "play your strong suit, right?" The three drifted slowly into their classroom. "I read that in a *Miss Teen* magazine. 'Turn your liabilities into assets.' "

"You're a real friend, Erica," Stephanie said. "*So* reassuring."

Down the hall, Arthur ambled up to Yick, who was stirring vaguely through the heap of uncatalogued junk on the floor of his locker. Yick and Arthur were both in grade seven, in Ms. Avery's class. Yick was slight, wiry and Chinese. Arthur was taller, curly-blonde and still a bit baby-fat. Arthur also had relations in high places, although it

7

didn't do him much good. Stephanie Kaye, class president, was his sister, but she had threatened him with a sudden, grisly death if he so much as breathed the information at school. Being in grade eight, she found it preferable, socially speaking, not to acknowledge Arthur. She was able to disown him because their parents were divorced; Stephanie lived with her mother, and used her mother's last name. Arthur, who lived with his father, was known as Arthur Kobalewsky.

"Hi, Yick," Arthur said. "Happy New Year."

Yick peered up at Arthur. "Hi, Arthur," he said. "Same here." He began rooting again in the locker, but as he did so, he dislodged the broken-off handle of a hockey stick at the back. Arthur watched it tilt slowly forward. Then from the end something large and pale and hairy dropped straight onto the back of Yick's neck. Yick slapped at it in irritation, but when he caught sight of it, he made a spectacular leap backward that carried him all the way across the hall, and just missed flattening Susie Rivera.

"What *is* that?" he gasped.

Arthur peered at the motionless object. "It sort of looks like a coonskin cap. What did you think it was?"

Yick advanced cautiously. "I thought it was a ghost. What's it doing there?"

"A ghost?" Arthur picked the thing up and examined it. It was a hat made out of matted, silvery gray shag. Inside, on a plastic liner printed to look like birch bark, were stamped the words, "Tennessee B'ar Killer."

"Ghosts aren't hairy."

"They are in Vietnam," said Yick. "Sometimes, anyway, they have long white hair, and they hop up and down. They try to get on your back and suck your blood."

"Hey, take it easy. It was just your hat," Arthur said. "Nothing to worry about." He handed it back to Yick, but Yick shook his head.

"I've never seen it before," he said, backing away nervously. "You take it, okay? Throw it away if you don't want it."

"You've never seen it before?" Considering the amount of stuff stored in his locker, Arthur supposed it was possible. Probably even Einstein couldn't remember all the things in Yick's locker. "Uh, so," Arthur said, stuffing the hat in his pocket, "what did you get for Christmas?"

"Firecrackers," Yick said, and tried unsuccessfully to close the locker door on the mess that was now threatening to spill out across the hallway.

"Firecrackers?" Arthur lived with his father, who could be eccentric sometimes, but he had never given anyone firecrackers for Christmas.

Yick kicked at the mess, and then wedged

9

the handle of his locker home, though the bottom corner still gaped open. "Yeah," he said. "We don't actually celebrate Christmas, but my grandfather gave me some firecrackers to save for New Year's."

"You set off firecrackers? At New Year's?" Yick's holidays were definitely unusual.

"Oh, yeah," said Yick, "but not this New Year. Our New Year comes in February."

"So what did you do over the holidays?" The two turned and began to walk toward their classroom.

"Oh, hung around the house, watched TV, visited relatives, and ate a ton of food."

"Same here," said Arthur. "Maybe you *do* celebrate Christmas."

"Are you all right, LD?" Voula was turned around in her seat, staring anxiously into LD's face.

"Huh? Oh, yeah, sure. Why?"

"Well, you're still wearing your coat. Are you cold or something?"

LD looked down at herself with a jolt of recognition. "Ah . . . no. No. I just got here, that's all. I didn't want to be late." She began to take off her coat, and realized she was still wearing her scarf and earmuffs as well. At least her mittens were in her pocket instead of on her hands. She must have looked like a complete broomhead, sitting there. She looked around the grade eight classroom and felt her face getting hot with embarrassment. "Maybe I've got time to hang these things in my locker."

"Sure," Voula said. "If Mr. Raditch asks about you, I'll tell him you'll be right back."

But Mr. Raditch came in just as LD was going out. "Leaving already?" he said, looking at the coat in her arms.

"I'm just going to hang this up," she muttered. Mr. Raditch stood aside to let her pass. Shaking his head slightly, he turned toward the front of the room, automatically removing Joey Jeremiah's hat as he did so.

"Good morning, class!" Ms. Avery beamed at the room full of grade sevens. "I hope you all had a good holiday. And I hope you are all well rested, because this term we will be working on a very large project." She paused and looked at them, sparking with anticipation. The grade sevens began to sit up straight as her electricity spread through the room.

"The entire school is going to work together," Ms. Avery continued, "to put on a play." She paused to let the effect sink in, and her dark eyes snapped with excitement. Arthur's hand went up. "Yes, Arthur?"

"You mean a real play? On stage?"

"That's what I mean. A four-day run in the school auditorium, with student actors and our own sets, and we'll sell tickets in

11

the neighborhood. We'll need every willing hand," she said, "because there is a tremendous amount of work involved. Everything from building sets to taking tickets, from sewing costumes to hanging lights. Even people to sell pop during the intermissions. So if you want to get involved, you can."

Meanwhile, Mr. Raditch had been introducing the same idea to his class. "I should point out," he concluded, "that as an added incentive, we have decided to allow up to twenty per cent of this term's mark for taking part in the play. So I strongly recommend it—especially for Certain Borderline Cases." His gaze swept around the room, and the face of every student suddenly became very thoughtful.

CHAPTER 2

For most of the students of Degrassi Junior High, the rest of the morning passed in a theatrical dream. In the hubbub of changing classes, Joey Jeremiah declared, "Wheels, my man, you are looking at Degrassi's number one dramatic talent. I mean, *the* gift to the stage."

"You going to audition?" Wheels, sandy haired, good looking and easy going, had learned long ago that the best way to deal with Joey's manic obsessions was to stand back and give them room.

"I've got to! It's their only hope of success! What about you?"

Wheels shrugged. "Yeah, I think I might try out for a part. How about you, Snake?"

Probing the shelf in his locker in search of a pen that worked, Snake, tall and thin as his namesake, shook his head. "I don't think so. I might help out backstage, though. Lights or sound or something like that."

Joey's eyes lit up like a pin-ball machine on grand-slam bonus. "Sound! That's it, Snake! You're a genius! It's got to be a musical!"

Snake looked dubious. "Like 'Sound of Music'?"

"Like 'Tommy,' bristle-brain! A rock opera! If it is, they'll need a band."

Wheels nodded appreciatively. "Hey, this could be our big chance."

Joey's hand traced a bright marquee in the air. "Degrassi performs Rock Opera of the Century! Starring JJ and the Jackrabbits! Albums available in the lobby!"

"Not unless we rehearse some more," Wheels said. "Besides, we haven't got a name yet — unless you've agreed to 'One Wheel Drive.' "

Joey groaned. "Why don't you just call it 'The Broken Cars'? Or 'Missing on Three Cylinders'?"

Snake closed his locker. "You guys are way off track," he said. " 'Snake and the Rattlers.' That's a name with bite."

Just then Erica, Heather and Stephanie walked by and the three boys put conversation on hold for a moment. Sensing their attention, the girls sang out, "Hi, boys!"

As if with one voice, they replied, "Hi, girls!"

14

"Hey, Steph! You going to try out for the play?" Snake called after them.

Stephanie flashed him a dazzling smile. "Am I? Of course!"

In fact, the school play seemed like a chance sent from heaven for Stephanie. If she wanted to change, what better way to do it than become an actress? Already she saw herself with a new identity: shy and elusive by day (dark glasses, and a soft felt hat pulled low to hide her face), but at night, on stage, holding a packed house breathless with her performance. As she lifted one white arm toward the floodlights, a gasp of appreciation swept through the audience. Slowly she tilted her head back, a gesture of submission to the tragedy of life. One shining tear slid down her cheek. As the curtain dropped, the audience roared its approval . . .

But not everyone was thinking of the play. LD was too preoccupied with the drama she imagined was unfolding at that very moment at the garage. She did think of skipping out of classes and going home, but the truth was, she was afraid to. She did not want to repeat the day she had come home and found that her father had been taken to the hospital. So she sat woodenly in her desk, hearing nothing, changing classes only because everyone around her did.

Arthur surveyed the library shelf carefully, his brows drawn together in concentration.

"I still don't see why you want to be in the play," Yick said. He was standing beside Arthur, paging through a book on the history of firearms.

"I think it could be very educational," Arthur said. "I might even consider a career on the stage. And besides, I could use the twenty per cent. Why don't you want to, Yick?"

"Me get up on stage? No way! Anyway, what's the point? There won't be any Chinese parts."

"But Ms. Avery said anyone who tried out would get *some* part." He pulled out a battered copy of *Macbeth*. "This has to be the play," he declared. "It's the only one we have more than one copy of." He cocked his head to read the titles on the spines.

"Even three copies won't go very far, though. I guess we'll have to share, or something."

Yick looked over his shoulder. "*Macbeth*," he said. "That's Scotland, isn't it? Lots of Chinese parts in that, I bet. MacYick MacYu."

"Well, there might be one, if you tried out for the play," Arthur said philosophically. "I wonder what 'exeunt' means?"

"Hello, LD. What can I do for you?" Doris

Bell, the school secretary, looked up from her typewriter.

"Can I use the phone, Miss Bell? I need to phone home."

"Help yourself, dearie."

LD deposited her books on the counter and pulled the phone to her. She dialed the number and waited. After the third ring, her dad's assistant, Jeff, answered. "Delacorte Garage."

LD suddenly found it impossible to speak. "Hello? Delacorte Garage. Anybody there?" She had been hoping her dad would answer — just the sound of his voice would tell her if he was all right. Lips pressed tight, she quietly hung up the receiver and pushed the phone back across the counter.

"Nobody there?" Doris asked as LD turned to go.

"Probably just outside," LD said. "Pumping gas for someone. Yeah, that's where he is."

Lucy, Voula, Erica and Heather sat in the library, discussing the play.

"The stage is a noble calling," Voula said with a faraway look in her eyes. "It was sacred to the ancient Greeks. In fact, my great-great-great-grandparents may have played to the gods! This play could be the most important thing in our lives." Behind her glasses, her dark, long-lashed, Mediterranean eyes shone with enthusiasm.

"Are you going to audition?" asked Erica.

"Oh, I would love to have a part," Voula said. "but only a small one."

"Why only a small one?" Lucy asked. "If you're going to go for it, you should go for the lead."

"I don't think I could be the lead," Voula said seriously, "but you could, Lucy. You know how to dance, and you took acting classes, didn't you?"

"Well ... yeah, I did. When we lived in New York."

"What do you do in acting class?" asked Heather.

"Did you meet any good-looking actors?" demanded Erica.

"Erica!" Heather dug her elbow into her sister's ribs.

"Well? I want to know."

"Sometimes," Lucy admitted. "I met a few cute guys there. Mostly it was girls and we did movement exercises and improvs — stuff like that."

"What's an improv?" Heather asked.

"Improvisation, dummy," said Erica.

"I know that," said Heather, "but what does it mean?"

"It means making a scene up as you go along," Lucy told her. "Like, suppose I say, anything blue is poison, but if you have something red, it keeps you alive."

The twins looked at each other. Erica was wearing a blue top. Heather's sweater was brown, but the collar of a blue shirt peeped out at her throat. A red pencil lay on the table in front of them. They dove for the pencil at the same instant and collided solidly. After a brief scuffle, Erica emerged the victor.

"No fair," Heather said. "What about me?"

Lucy had been watching them closely. Now she said, "You're dying. You have to show me you're getting weaker."

Heather began to gasp and crumple. Just before she slid out of her chair, she stretched an imploring hand toward Erica. Erica was on the point of relenting and sharing the red pencil with her sister, but Heather was enjoying an agonizing death. With a horrible gurgle, she sank to the floor. When she looked up from the carpet, however, she found everyone in the library staring at her.

"Here." Erica tried to tuck the pencil behind her ear. "This will make you feel better."

"Quit it," said Heather, scrambling back into her chair, her face flushed a deep crimson.

"You should try out for the play," Voula told Heather, but Heather shook her head.

"Actually," she said, "we were thinking of doing make-up."

"I'm hoping the play will be *Return of the*

19

Slime," Erica said with relish. "We've made some great Hallowe'en costumes, and slime is my specialty. I'm pretty good on eyeballs, too."

"Completely gross," agreed Heather. "My specialty is scars."

"Um, it sounds — wonderful," Voula said. "But, Lucy, you *have* to try out for the play. You know so much about the theater."

"Maybe," Lucy said. "I don't know."

"But why not?" Voula demanded.

"Actually, it depends on what the play is," Lucy said with an air of long-suffering sophistication. "If it was real theater, I would. But it'll probably be some stuffy old Victorian farce. You know — a house full of butlers, where everyone's rich? Nobody lives like that!"

CHAPTER 3

LD offered the salad bowl to her father for a third time. "You sure you don't want some?" she said. "It's good for you."

Frank Delacorte looked at his daughter in surprise. "LD," he said, "I'm the father. I'm supposed to get you to eat salad. Which I notice you didn't do."

LD looked down at her plate, where her food lay practically untouched. "I'm not hungry, I guess. Dad?"

"Yes?"

"How come you were all dressed up this morning?"

"Oh, I . . . had to go downtown for an appointment. Did it surprise you?"

"Yeah, sort of."

"I should wear that suit more often. Suits aren't just to be buried in, you know." He leaned back in his chair and looked at her for a moment.

His hair is so gray, LD thought. When did it get so gray? She saw fine, crow's-foot wrinkles at the corners of his eyes. He's getting old, she thought — or is there something wrong with him?

"Someday," her father was saying, "I hope you remember your father was more than just a grease monkey."

LD's eyes widened. "What do you mean — remember?"

"Well, I'm not going to live forever, am I?"

"Don't say that! Don't!"

"Hey, take it easy, LD. All right, forget I said anything. Maybe I *will* live forever." And he peered at his reflection in the chrome of the toaster, smoothed his hair, and chuckled.

But later, while she cleared the table and made him a pot of tea, he said, seriously, "So, you can take care of yourself pretty good now, can't you?"

The words set off fire bells inside her head, but she only said, "Maybe. I don't know. Why?"

"I mean, you're a big girl now. If I left you alone, you'd be all right. If Jeff could stay here, you — " But he was interrupted by the telephone.

When he went to answer it, LD let her forehead sink down against the cool enamel of the refrigerator. "What is going on?" she murmured. "What's happening . . . ?"

A few minutes later, he came back, drained his teacup and said, "Sorry, LD, I've got to go give Mr. Munro a boost. I'll be back in a little while."

"I'll go!" She blurted the words without thinking.

"To boost a dead battery?" He frowned. "LD, you can't drive the truck."

"Well, let me come with you. I could do it for you."

"LD," he said, "it's time you thought about something besides the garage. It isn't always going to be so important to you, you know. Believe me, I know what I'm talking about. You've got big changes ahead of you . . ."

"Oh, stop talking about changes!" LD shouted. "I can't stand it!" Then under her father's startled gaze, she snatched up her coat and said, "I have to go out, too. I'm doing homework at Voula's."

Arthur sat in his room with the copy of *Macbeth* open before him. Looking away from the book, he tried to remember the lines. "So foul and — " He looked down. " — fair. So foul and fair a day I — " He looked again. "So foul and fair a day I have not — uh — seen." He was not entirely sure what that meant, but he hoped it would get clearer as he went on.

Then he remembered what Yick had said. The play was in Scotland, so probably he should be talking like a Scot. That meant rolling his *r*'s, which he had never been very good at. Fortunately there was only one, so far. He tried again.

"So foul and fairrrrrrrr ... " The *r* wouldn't roll. He tried again. "So foul and ..." He took a deep breath and threw his tongue so far back in his throat he almost swallowed it. " — fai-urk-glug!" He ducked forward and held his throat, but his tongue had given up trying to descend to his stomach. Gingerly, he started again. "So foul and fairrrrr ... " The *r* stayed as level as a pool table, so finally he tried giving it a little curl at the end, instead of in the middle. " ... fairuh ... fairuh ... So foul and fairuh uh day ... " He looked at the book. " ... I have not seen." He stood up, struck a pose in front of the mirror, and tried it once more for effect. Squaring his shoulders and looking as much as he could like a Scottish knight, he declaimed, "So foul and fairuh uh day I have not seen."

Not bad, he thought. Not bad at all. Now for the rest of the play.

LD was walking fast down the empty street, her fists shoved in her pockets and her head bowed into the wind. She hadn't meant to come out, and she had no plan to go to Voula's. She just had to get away from her father. Unwanted phrases floated through her mind: *"If I left you alone, you'd be all right . . . big changes coming . . . I'm not going to live forever, you know . . . "* She walked even faster to escape these thoughts, turning corners and crossing streets at random.

When at last she slowed down, she found, to her surprise, that she was on Voula's street after all. She might as well call on her. At least she would be able to honestly tell her father she had been here. She turned in at the gate and rang the bell.

After what seemed a long time, she saw a light come on behind the rippled glass. Voula's father opened the door.

"Hello?" he said.

"Is Voula here?"

"She's doing her homework."

"I — I have to ask her a question about homework. I'm in her class."

"You didn't phone?"

"I was walking by, and just thought of it."

For a moment LD thought he was going to refuse to let her even talk to Voula, but suddenly he held the door open wide and said, "Come in." Then he called up the stairs, "Voula! Someone is here." While they waited for Voula to appear, he studied her, with particular attention to her blue cap. "It's late for a young girl to be out walking. Does your father know?"

"Y — yes, he knows."

Then Voula came down the stairs to her rescue. "LD!" she said. "Hi! Papa, this is LD. You remember, she's in my class."

Voula's father nodded to LD. "Okay," he said to Voula, "don't talk too long. You should finish your homework and go to bed."

When they were standing alone in the hall, Voula said, "Is everything okay, LD?"

"I guess so. I sort of blew up at my dad and said I was coming over here to study."

"What did you blow up at him for?"

"Oh — I don't know. He keeps talking as if he's going away. It scares me."

Voula's dark eyes widened. "You think it's his heart? Is there something he hasn't told you?"

"Well . . . yeah. I don't know what else to think."

"Oh, LD! What are you going to do?"

"What can I do? I try to take care of him, but he goes on just the same. And he doesn't want me around much, either."

"What do you mean?"

"He doesn't want me to help in the garage — says I've got changes coming. It's like he's trying to prepare me for something." Voula stared wordlessly at her. "Look," LD said, "I should go before I get you in trouble. Did we have any homework?"

"Just studying for the test."

LD felt a small black hole opening up beneath her feet. "Test?"

"From Mr. Raditch. Weren't you listening? He went on and on about it."

"No, I guess I wasn't," LD said. "I better go home and study."

"It's on prefixes and suffixes," Voula said as she walked out onto the porch. "Good luck."

Somehow, as she headed down the stairs and turned for home, LD doubted she would be able to concentrate much.

CHAPTER 4

"Good morning, class," Ms. Avery said. "Before we begin, I have more details for you about the play." Everyone inched forward in anticipation.

"We're going to start auditions tomorrow," Ms. Avery went on. "Anyone who wants to try out should put their name down on the list I'm going to leave in the office. And I'm going to leave another list there of jobs behind the scenes and at the front of the house. That means things like taking tickets and checking coats. Remember, these jobs are every bit as important. Without them, the curtain would never go up. It's going to be a lot of work — probably staying after school one or two nights a week, and maybe even on weekends. And of course you would have to be available for the four nights of performance in February. But it's going to be a lot of fun, too. So I hope you will all put your names down for something. If we all work together, we can make this a big success."

Kathleen put her hand up. "Yes, Kathleen."

"Ms. Avery, what kind of play will it be?"

"That's a good question, Kathleen. I think we have the resources to do a play called *Blood and Moonlight*. It's actually a very serious play about young people like yourselves, growing up poor in the middle of a city. Sort of like around here, but much tougher and poorer. It would be a big challenge, but I think we could do it."

"Are there any love scenes in it?" At Kathleen's question, glances ricocheted among the other students, and someone smothered a giggle.

Ms. Avery perched herself on the edge of her desk. "No. A love triangle, yes. And there is a lot of deep feeling. But I'm sorry to tell you there are no love scenes. I hope you all won't be too disappointed."

The class dissolved in laughter. When it subsided, Ms. Avery said, "Remember — the two lists will be in the office. Put your names down, and we'll put together the best play this school has ever seen."

Lucy and Steph met in the girls' washroom. Stephanie was staring at her reflection again, with her hair pulled back in one hand, wondering if she was really as scrawny and ugly as she felt.

"Hi, Steph," Lucy said as she came in. "You're different this term. How come?"

"I'm trying to change my look. I don't know if it's working, though."

"Trying to dodge Joey? I noticed he hasn't been bugging you as much as last term."

"Oh, no," Steph said. "It's nothing to do with him. I don't care one way or the other about Joey. I just felt it was, you know, time to try something different."

"I know what you mean," Lucy said. "I had a long talk with my social worker about that last night."

"Yeah?"

"Yeah, my court date comes up in March." Although she was better off than most kids in school, Lucy had been picked up for shoplifting before Christmas, and the police had decided to charge her. Now she had a family counsellor, scheduled time with her parents, a social worker, a lawyer and the cloud of a court appearance looming on the horizon. "She thinks it would be a good idea if I got involved in things here at school. To change my look." She laughed without humor. "Seems like how you look matters more than what you do."

"Oh, yeah, the system," Steph said, though she didn't know if she agreed with Lucy or not. "Get involved with what kind of things?"

"I told her about the play, and she said I should try out for it. Even if it was *Goldilocks and the Three Bears*." She wrinkled her nose. "I'm so glad it's going to be *Blood and Moonlight*."

"You know it?"

"Oh, yeah. It's great. Real strong off-off-Broadway. The part of Carmen is completely electric."

"Who's Carmen?"

"She's the female lead. Young, tough, sensitive, dedicated to her boyfriend, even though he's under a lot of pressure from the street-gang, the Cannibals. You should try out for the part. When we went to see it produced in the village, the woman who played her looked a lot like you."

Stephanie felt a thrill shoot through her, from her scalp to the soles of her feet. "Really? Like *me*?"

"She could have been your sister. But I mean you like you are now. Not the way you used to be . . . "

A moment later, Stephanie floated from the washroom, and walked, with the calm dignity and grace of those who have heard their life's calling, to the office to sign up for an audition. She felt some compassion for the other names already on the list, but she knew they would all get bit parts, at least. Maybe even a supporting role. Very deliberately she signed her name, but instead of dotting the 'i' in Stephanie, she drew a tiny star. It was, she thought, her first autograph. Some day, it would be worth a fortune.

Arthur sighed deeply as he returned the copy of *Macbeth* to the library. "I think Shakespeare must be an acquired taste," he said to Yick. "And I haven't acquired it yet."

"Too bad," Yick said. "I was looking forward to seeing you in a kilt. So, are you still going to try out for the play?"

"Of course," Arthur replied.

Together they walked to the office. When they came through the door, Doris said, "More heartbreakers!"

"Actually, Miss Bell," Arthur said, "we're here to sign up for the play."

"That's what I mean. Wild and handsome young things breaking the hearts of every girl in the audience."

Arthur looked behind him, but only Yick was there. "Uh, where do we sign?" he asked nervously. He had noticed before that adults could display sudden bursts of irrationality. At such times, it was best to humor them.

"The clipboard on the left is for auditions. The one on the right is for crew and front of house," Doris said, and went back to her typing.

While Arthur carefully printed his name, Yick looked over the other clipboard. "Hey!"

he said suddenly. "This play has special effects."

"What kind of special effects?"

"It doesn't say, but I'm going to sign up for it anyway."

"What do you know about special effects?" asked Arthur. "Isn't that sawing women in half and cars blowing up?"

Yick took the pen from Arthur's hand and wrote his name on the list. "I'm Chinese. We invented gunpowder, you know."

"If you say so," Arthur said. "I hope the school has insurance. I can tell this is going to be some play."

CHAPTER 5

The students waiting their turns to audition sat nervously around the library, staring at the scripts they had been given. All except Stephanie, that is. Stephanie looked pityingly at the others, and thought about her future. After the play she would probably be offered a part in a movie, but she knew already she didn't want to have anything to do with those juvenile *Dizzy's Diner* films. I mean, who wants to throw pies and get squirted with catsup all the time? No, it would have to be something artistic, or she just wouldn't take it . . .

Susie came to the door and consulted a sheet of paper. "Melanie? You're next."

As Melanie got up, looking flustered, Caitlyn said, "Good luck!" and Rick called out, "Go for it, Melanie!" Then she went out with

Susie, who walked her down the hall to the classroom where Ms. Avery and Mr. Raditch were holding the auditions.

Lucy, sitting across from Stephanie, looked up from the script she had been reading. "I hate auditions. Going on stage is nothing compared to this."

"Oh, yeah," said Steph, checking out her nails. "I know what you mean."

"You do?" said Lucy. "I didn't know you'd acted before."

"Uh . . . sure," Stephanie said, startled. "I . . . sure, but not for years." She dimly remembered a Christmas play in grade three that kept it from being a complete lie. "What part do you think you'll get?" she asked quickly.

"I figure I might as well shoot for the top," Lucy said. "I want to read for Carmen."

"Ca-Carmen?" Steph said. "You mean, the lead?"

"Sure," Lucy said. "Why not? I think I've got as good a chance as anybody. What about you?"

"I . . . anything, I guess. The, uh . . . " Stephanie checked the script lying on the table in front of her. "The social worker or, uh, the teacher . . . or Carmen," she finished defiantly. Hadn't Lucy said she was perfect for Carmen? Why was she trying to get Stephanie's part?

"You've got a good attitude," Lucy said. "Keeps you from being disappointed. And it's going to be a gas to do, no matter what part we get."

Just then Susie came back. "Stephanie?" she said, looking at her list.

The calm of a few moments before was gone now. With a surge of alarm, Stephanie rose to her feet, somehow getting tangled with her chair as she did so. When at last she was free, she turned toward the door, but Lucy called after her, "Don't forget your script."

"Oh, yeah. Thanks," mumbled Steph.

"And good luck. Break a leg."

"Right." Stephanie filed the expression for later examination, and followed Susie out of the room.

Ms. Avery and Mr. Raditch sat in students' desks in the front row, with pads of yellow paper covered with scribbles. The teacher's desk had been pushed into one corner, making an open area in front of them. Stephanie dimly heard the door close behind her, but her ears were filled with a thundering roar. Spots swam in front of her eyes.

"Hello, Stephanie," Ms. Avery said with a welcoming smile. "How are you today?"

"F-i- . . . " Stephanie's voice had become like crumpled paper stuck in her throat. Frantically, she swallowed and tried again. "Fine!" she blurted. They were going to think she was a total sockhead.

"I'm glad you want to be in the play," Ms. Avery said. "We can certainly use you. Did you have a particular part you want to try for?"

"Well . . . Carmen?"

"Mm-hmm." Ms. Avery made a note on her pad, and then said, "Then let's try Act Two, Scene Three — that's page twenty-two of your script, Stephanie. Mr. Raditch will read the part of Eddy. Just forget who he is, and try to think of him as your own age."

Mr. Raditch smiled wryly, and Steph laughed nervously. "Then, whenever you're ready . . . " Ms. Avery was saying.

Stephanie stared at the script, and found Carmen's first speech at the top of the page. "Eddy," she said woodenly, "is that you?"

"Yeah, it's me," Mr. Raditch said, making his voice sound rough. "What are you doing here?"

"I been waitin' for you," Steph said. "I knew you would come." She felt waves of embarrassment rolling over her at the thought of waiting for Mr. Raditch.

"I told you not to come round here anymore, Carmen. I told you to forget we ever met."

Stephanie had been staring at the page, but she looked up for a moment, and found that Mr. Raditch was looking at her while he spoke. In confusion, she lost her place. "I been wait . . . no. Uh, I ain't like that, Eddy.

37

I can't just forget you like that." She felt her cheeks begin to flame. "You mean too much to me."

"If I mean anything at all to you, Carmen, you'll just clear out of here. Get out of this whole rotten city!"

"But, Eddy, I — "

"I mean it, Carmen!" Mr. Raditch cut in with surprising force. "This place is poison and so am I!"

According to the script, Eddy left Carmen alone at this point. Stephanie looked up at Ms. Avery.

"Keep going," Ms. Avery said. "Read Carmen's monologue. Take your time. And remember, Carmen here is talking about her first love — the first thing that has ever made her life worthwhile."

Stephanie looked at the speech for a moment, and then began. "Sure. That makes a lot of sense, doesn't it? All my life I been here in this city, with nothing but rats and rust and roaches — " She made a face but kept on going. " — with peeling paint and holes in the windows, no money, not enough to eat and someone waiting to rip you off if you ever get anything special — " Stephanie felt the speech beginning to take hold. Her voice was getting stronger, and she was only dimly aware of Ms. Avery and Mr. Raditch. She felt the tragedy of growing up in a harsh world, like a flower through a crack in the concrete. " — and the only thing that ever kept me going was sometimes I would see the moon shining above the project. Once I saw it after a rainstorm, when everything seemed clean for a change, and the clouds were blown apart by the wind. It was beautiful! So I watched for it all the time, and I knew, deep inside I *knew* someday the moon is going to give me somebody to love. And then it does. The first time I seen Eddy, I knew he was the one. It was like there was a little bit of moonlight shinin' down on *him*, and it didn't matter he was sitting in some scummy tenement hallway flipping nickels with Sharkey McGriff. He was the one. And so what happens? Suddenly he doesn't want to see me no more. That makes a whole lot of sense."

She lowered the page and looked up. Ms. Avery and Mr. Raditch had been watching her closely. Now they smiled and gently applauded. Stephanie felt a huge wave of relief ripple through her.

"Thank you, Stephanie. That was very good," Ms. Avery said. "Quite satisfactory."

"You mean, I can have the part?"

"Oh, I can't say that yet. We have to give everyone a chance. We'll know tomorrow, or the next day at the latest."

"Oh."

Ms. Avery smiled again. "Okay? Please tell Susie we're ready for the next one on her list. We'll see you later."

Numbly, Stephanie stumbled out the door

and down the hall, not sure whether she should be depressed or jubilant. They didn't say no — and they did applaud. But maybe they did that for everyone. Then she remembered doing the scene with Mr. Raditch and felt her skin start to creep. That was so gross! Of course, if she did get the part it wouldn't be with Mr. Raditch. But maybe it would be with Wheels! She knew he was going to try for a part.

Completely captured by this possibility, she walked right by Susie without delivering her message. Fortunately, Susie didn't need to be told. Making a checkmark on her clipboard, she stepped into the library. "Lucy . . . ? Your turn now."

CHAPTER 6

"Attention, students," said the intercom. "You are reminded that it is forbidden to put foreign objects in cafeteria food until it has been purchased. Would the person responsible for the toy duck found in the pot of chili please report to the office immediately..."

Voula stopped at LD's locker. They hadn't really talked since LD had come by her house the other night. "Hi, LD. How's your dad?"

LD shrugged. "Okay, I guess. He seemed all right this morning. Unusually great, in fact. I don't know whether to worry, or if I'm just going crazy."

Voula looked blank. "Why would you worry about him looking great?"

"Because nothing seems normal anymore.

But then I've sort of forgotten what normal is. He says he's as strong as an ox," LD added irrelevantly.

Lucy's locker was two away from LD's. She stuck her head around the open door. "Is your dad sick again?" Her dark eyes registered concern.

"I don't know," LD said. "I can't tell. But he's been acting funny lately."

"Funny like how?" Lucy asked.

"Well . . . last night, he wanted me to look at old albums with him."

"Photo albums?" said Voula.

"Yeah, old family pictures. Of my brothers, and my mum. Even really old pictures of relatives in Corsica. They make me feel creepy. I mean, half of the people are dead already, and I've never met any of them. Who cares?"

"Why did he want to do that?" demanded Lucy.

LD shrugged and looked unhappy. "It's sort of like he wants to give me something — you know — while he can? I just have the feeling he's getting ready to — to leave . . . or something." LD closed her locker and there was a moment of uneasy silence among the three girls. Lucy broke it. "Look, LD, if you need anything, like, help or anything, we're your friends, right?"

"Yeah, thanks, Lucy," LD said. She looked at Voula. "Thanks."

"Good morning, scholars," Mr. Raditch said, and then noted a hand up at the back of the room. "Mr. Jeremiah?"

"Is the play cast yet, Mr. Raditch?"

"Anticipating fame, Mr. Jeremiah?"

"Hey, I got to plan my life, don't I?" He fended off the adoring crowds. "No autographs, please . . . " In a soft falsetto, Wheels said, "Ooh, it's him! It's him! Joey Jeremiah!"

"If I were you, Mr. Jeremiah," Mr. Raditch said drily, "I wouldn't give up learning to read and write. You may need those skills some day to get a job outside the theater. I believe Ms. Avery will post the cast list tomorrow. We saw many promising actors and actresses yesterday. I am also very pleased with the turnout for the technical side. However, there are some major openings unfilled, and there is still room for anyone who would like to volunteer."

He picked up a stack of test papers from his desk. "Now, about the test. Your papers contained the usual collection of pleasant and unpleasant surprises," Mr. Raditch said. "Some of you show an acceptable mastery of prefixes and suffixes, while others seem to have forgotten to come back from holidays." He began to pass out the tests. "Anyone who got less than sixty per cent on this should do some serious review. Otherwise you will have great difficulty with our next unit. Voula . . . very good . . . Mr. Jeremiah . . .

43

some very creative suggestions here, but on the whole, not bad ... " He continued until he reached the last paper, which he placed on his desk. "LD," he said. "See me after class."

LD dropped her gaze and stared hard at her desk. She already knew she had bombed out on the test — but it didn't really matter. It was just one more cloud in a very gloomy world.

As the classroom emptied, LD gathered her books and walked to Mr. Raditch's desk. Without a word, he handed her the test paper. At the top, in red pen, was written "10%!?!"

"What happened?" Mr. Raditch asked.

"I forgot to study, I guess."

"It looks like you forgot to do the test. Half of the questions are blank."

"Uh ... yeah ... I didn't know what to do."

"LD, is something wrong? This isn't like you."

"No ... I don't know ... "

She wished she was anywhere else, but Mr. Raditch wasn't finished yet. He gestured to a desk. "Sit down." He slid into the desk opposite. "Look, LD, I can tell something's bothering you. You haven't been yourself since you came back to school. Now, you don't have to tell me what it is, but if this goes on very long, you're going to make a lot of trouble for yourself. Is everything all right at home?"

LD's eyes shifted uneasily.

"How is your father?"

LD shrugged. Mr. Raditch looked steadily at her for a few moments, and then said, "Let me change the subject a bit, then. You didn't put your name down for the play."

"I can't act."

"You don't have to. We have a serious gap in our crew. I was hoping you might help out."

"Doing what?"

"Building sets. I know you're good with cars, and I think you could be a good carpenter, too. We need someone to oversee everything. To get the scenery built on time and make sure it doesn't collapse in the middle of a performance. To see that the lights get hung, and the special effects work. It's not very complicated compared to a V-8 engine, but it could be a lot of fun. What do you say?"

"Well . . . how much time would it take?"

"That depends on how fast everyone works. It would take some nights, and there might be some weekend work. And it's like being on a school team. You would have to keep your marks above water. But you would get extra credit."

But LD's thoughts were not on the sets, or the extra credit, or the fact that she had been asked to take charge of something. She was thinking of all the time the project would take — even weekends. She had found a hole to crawl into, and now she intended to pull it in after herself, so that no one, not even her father, could find her.

It took her only a few seconds to make a decision. "Sure. I'll do it."

CHAPTER   7

On her way to school the next day, Stephanie's stomach churned with anxiety. They would find out the casting for the play today. If she was lucky — *oh, please, let me be lucky*, she thought, and rolled her eyes toward the crisp blue winter sky — if she was lucky, she would have the part of Carmen, and Wheels, that dreamboat, would be Eddy, Carmen's lover. It was her only hope, she had decided. Last term she had tried every way she could think of to get something started between them, always with disastrous results. She had asked Wheels out, not once but *twice*, and both dates had —just by accident, really—turned into those horrible moments you would like to put in a time machine and send back to about two zillion B.C.

But nothing had changed the way she felt about Wheels. Now, if only they could play the parts of Eddy and Carmen, she just *knew* the fire would catch at last. The play had lots of possibilities. How could he say some of those things without, well, realizing they could apply to her, Stephanie Kaye? She crossed her fingers on both hands, rolled her eyes skyward again, and launched a silent plea.

When she got to school, she found there was a crowd of students knotted around a notice posted outside the school office. "Degrassi Junior High School Play — Meeting Backstage Today — 4 pm!!! *BRING YOUR SCRIPTS!* it said, and underneath there were two lists. Craning forward, Stephanie saw that one was for crew. The other, just glimpsed over the intervening heads, was for the cast. Pressing forward, she saw near the top of the list: "Eddy — Derek Wheeler." "He got it!" she squealed. "Wheels got it! Oh, thank you, thank you, thank you . . . "

The students in front glanced back at her outburst and edged cautiously aside. Not caring what they thought, she leaned forward and scanned the rest of the list. There it was! "Carm — " What? Stephanie stopped and read it again.

"Carmen — Lucy Baines." Stephanie's face crumpled. They gave the part to Lucy! She couldn't believe it. Didn't they know *she* looked just like Carmen? Lucy only wanted the part to satisfy her social worker! Shattered, she turned away. Dimly, behind her, she heard Joey Jeremiah exclaim, "Hey! Lucky me! I got the part of Lucky!" But Stephanie didn't want to hear about luck right now.

She ran into Lucy outside the girls' washroom. "Hi, Steph!" Lucy said. "Congratulations."

"Congratulations?" Stephanie said. "What for?"

"For getting the part," Lucy said. "Didn't you see the list? You got the part of Mrs. Wark, Carmen's mother."

"Her *mother?*"

"Yeah. It's a good character part, lots of meat in it. But I guess I'll have to call you Mom. I'm Carmen." Lucy laughed, and Stephanie feebly joined in. Not only had she lost her only chance of getting Wheels to look at her — she had to play the *mother* of his stage girlfriend.

When Lucy left, Stephanie went back down the hallway to have another look at the cast list. Yes, there was her name, just as Lucy had said — "Mrs. Wark — Stephanie Kaye." Who else got a part? Her eye ran down the list, but she could not remember what the parts were. Then she saw a line that made her freeze: "Chip — Arthur Kobalewsky." Arthur was her brother, her embarrassing little grade seven brother, but wasn't

Chip the name of . . . ? Frantically she scrabbled in her bag and pulled out her copy of the script. Then she collapsed against the wall with a groan of frustration. Yuck! Yuck! Yuck! Not only did she have to play an old woman while Lucy and Wheels were lovers, she had to be the mother of her own twirpy brother! Chip was Mrs. Wark's son.

When LD walked into the backstage room, she found it already packed. Voula was sitting on a shelf along one wall. "Here's a place," she waved, and made room for LD. "Isn't it exciting?"

"Yeah," LD said, looking around the room. "I guess so. I didn't realize there would be so many people."

"There's a big cast," Voula said. "Don't you wish you had a part, LD?"

LD snorted. "Me show my face on stage? No way!"

Ms. Avery had been checking names off on a list. Now she stood up and looked around the room. "All right. I think everyone is here. First of all, I want to welcome you all. You are the cast and crew of Degrassi Junior High's production of *Blood and Moonlight*." Spontaneous cheering erupted from the students jammed around her.

"Okay," Ms. Avery said, "settle down. We don't have a lot of time this afternoon, and

50

I've got a few things to say." She consulted her clipboard, and then went on. "First I'm going to introduce you to each other, and then I'm going to tell you the rules of the game. Then Mr. Raditch will have some things to say about the technical part of the production.

"I'm going to introduce the cast the way they will be listed in the program — in order of appearance. There are no stars in this production." She paused and surveyed everyone carefully. "You all deserve credit, and no one here is any more important than anyone else. Okay?" Ms. Avery paused again and several heads nodded in agreement.

"Then, the cast, in order of appearance, will be: Joey as Lucky Spoletti, Wheels as Eddy O'Toole, Alex as Arnold Fish. Those three characters hang around together, and Lucky — that's you, Joey, is the head of the local gang, the Cannibals." A voice from the back of the room said, "Oh, he's bad, real bad," and Joey pulled his hat down over his eyes to make himself look dangerous.

"Right," Ms. Avery said. "Then we meet Carmen Wark, who will be played by Lucy, and Angel Kaminski, played by Erica. Angel and Carmen are friends, but they become rivals for Eddy."

"That's me," Wheels said.

"I know," Ms. Avery said. "Ridiculous, isn't it?" Everyone laughed.

"Then the play takes us to Carmen's home

— a dingy, third-floor walk-up apartment — where we meet her mother, Mrs. Wark, played by Stephanie — " Stephanie sank visibly between Erica and Heather. " — a very challenging role," Ms. Avery added. "And we meet Carmen's brother Chip, played by Arthur, and her sister Rose, played by Melanie. Next on the scene is Carmen's schoolteacher, Mrs. Horace — that's Voula — followed by Annie as the next-door neighbor, Caitlyn as Miss Andrews, a social worker, and Rick as a policeman."

Ms. Avery looked up from her notes. "I'll be talking to the cast about the play in more detail, but while you're all here, I'll just say that this is a play about people who are poor. Life is hard for them. Their world is ugly and violent except for a few sparks of tenderness and courage — which prove stronger than the darkness, in the end. Now, Mr. Raditch, would you like to introduce the crew?"

Mr. Raditch stood up. "Thanks, Ms. Avery. We have some gaps in our crew, so people may double up and do several jobs, but I can tell you some of the jobs already. First of all, our stage manager is going to be Susie Rivera." Everyone turned and looked at Susie, who grinned self-consciously.

"A stage manager is a little like a traffic cop," Mr. Raditch went on. "She makes sure the right people are ready for rehearsals, and keeps things running smoothly. And when the play is actually being performed, she gives the cues — tells everyone when to start, in other words, and prompts them if they forget their lines. So when Susie tells you something, I expect you to listen." There were calls of "Aye-aye, captain!" from the back row, and Joey gave Susie a boy scout salute. Mr. Raditch continued, "We are also going to ask Susie to be Lucy's understudy. She will learn Lucy's part, just in case Lucy can't perform for some reason.

"Other backstage jobs, all equally important, are: LD as our master carpenter and general head of construction, Snake in charge of lights and sound, Heather and Erica doing make-up, Spike and Annie, costumes, and Yick, special effects."

At this Wheels said, "Do I need a catcher's mask or what?!"

"How about a flak jacket?" Joey added.

Mr. Raditch took no notice. "We haven't got our front of house staff worked out yet," he said. "That means ushers, ticket takers, coat checkers and so on, but that will come. For now, Kathleen will be in charge of that area." He looked around at Ms. Avery. "That's it for me, right now."

Ms. Avery said, "This is a big project, and it's going to take a lot of work, responsibility and maturity. It's also going to be a lot of fun, and I'm looking forward to it. Any questions?"

There were none. "All right, then," she

said. "Crew, Mr. Raditch wants to meet with you right now in the carpentry shop. Cast, you stay here with me, and we'll figure out a rehearsal schedule."

As if a trance had been broken, all the students began to move and talk at once. Although opening night was almost two months away, the countdown to performance had begun.

CHAPTER 8

The technical crew ranged itself around a work table in the carpentry shop, where a line of gray machine tools slumbered along one wall, and the sweet dusty memory of sawn wood filled the air. Back in one corner sat a jumble of sets from productions in years gone by. Amongst them, LD saw a Santa Claus fireplace, complete with faded felt stocking, and a two-dimensional tree with a painted owl in its branches.

"Okay," said Mr. Raditch. "First of all, I want to say that I will not be riding herd on you, unless you develop bad habits like cutting your arms and legs off with the table saw. This play should be put together by students. I will be available to you if you need advice. But it's up to you to make it all work. And so, I have asked LD to be the head of construction."

Everyone turned and looked at her, and LD felt her face growing warm. She had not realized she was going to be responsible for *everyone*. She grinned uncertainly.

"Now," Mr. Raditch went on, "before I fade into the background, I'm going to point out some of the technical problems you will have to solve to make this play work. First, the easy parts." He looked at Annie and Spike. "Costumes will be simple — ordinary clothes like jeans and t-shirts, but worn out. You'll have to borrow a uniform for Rick, and you'll need a couple of Cannibal crests." Annie scribbled a note, and Mr. Raditch continued, "Heather, there is nothing unusual in make-up, except for Arnold's blood in Act Five. Lights will be straightforward, too, Snake, but you'll need some convincing moonlight. Sets don't need to be fancy, either. But the number of sets is a problem, and you will have to think of something for that."

"What kind of problem?" LD said.

"Well, the usual way to change scenes is with flies. You hang your set on a fly, and pull it up out of sight when you don't need it. But we have only three flies here, and there are five scenes. So you will have to find a simple way to change scenes without breaking up the action. Maybe see if there are ways we can use parts of one scene in another. We have a very small budget, and limited labor. So we need to look for ways of making something out of nothing and using it twice."

He looked at Yick. "And the other place where you will need some ingenuity is in special effects."

Yick pushed his glasses up on his nose and looked alert. "Yes, sir."

"Now, we don't want to make this too complicated," Mr. Raditch said, "but there are a few places in the play where the right effect can perk the whole production up. I've made a little list ... " He consulted his notes. "There is a distant police siren in Act One — you will have to work with Snake on that one — and there is another siren in Act Five, much closer, with flashing police lights. Snake, at that point, if you can get a tape of a police radio and play it, that will help. There are gunshots off stage in Act Five — we should be able to use a starter's pistol for that, but you may have to experiment a little to get the right sound — maybe shoot into a garbage can or something like that. But all those are fairly easy. The one that will give you the most trouble, I think, will be the ghost in Act Four."

Yick's smile of anticipation froze. "Ghost? What ghost?"

"Haven't you read the play?" Mr. Raditch asked. "In Act Four, Eddy sees the ghost of Sharkey the Stiff. That's what makes him change his mind about going on the raid with Lucky. So we have to come up with a convincing spook. Something really hair-raising," he said with relish.

"Couldn't we do without a ghost?" Yick asked nervously.

"If we don't have a ghost," Mr. Raditch said, "it's going to look like Wheels is having a hallucination. It would change the play quite a bit." Mr. Raditch looked at his watch. "We're almost out of time. You'll have to carry on next week. But LD is in charge. When do you meet again, LD?"

"Ah . . . as soon as we can, I guess," LD said. "The same time Monday?"

Everyone nodded. "You're the boss," Snake said.

"Okay," LD said. "Monday it is. And, uh, be ready to work."

"Does everyone have a copy of the script?" Ms. Avery asked, when the crew had swirled away and left the room in comparative quiet. There was a general nodding of heads. "Good," she said. "Guard it with your life. Until you have your parts memorized, you will be making notes on your script, so if you lose it, a lot of work goes down the drain. Now, I'm going to pass around a sheet, and I want you to put down your name and any days or times you *regularly* can't come to a rehearsal. That includes things like paper routes, or team practices. I know some of you are on sports teams."

"What about detentions?" asked Joey.

"Just *regularly* scheduled events," replied Ms. Avery. "It hasn't got that bad yet, has it, Joey?"

Joey grinned. "Not yet, Ms. Avery."

While Ms. Avery ran through the ground rules, the students began to realize, each in his own way, that the world was about to change — by light years. To follow Ms. Avery's talk, Wheels had to ignore a steady stream of cracks and one-liners from Joey, who was wound up tight with excitement. Wheels was excited, too, but he had looked at the script, and he was aware that the play drew a line between his character and Joey's. Joey's character, Lucky, turned out to be a thief, a dealer and a double-crosser, while Wheels' character, Eddy, tried to go straight. Already, Wheels felt himself leaning away from Joey. Besides, he wanted to think about Eddy's relationship with Carmen. He'd never really looked at Lucy before . . .

Stephanie sat woodenly through Ms. Avery's remarks about rehearsals. She was still coming to grips with the idea of being an old woman — that was how she thought of the mother in the play. It was as if all the other students in the play were going to have a party, and she had to be the chaperone, reminding them to turn the music down and be home by nine. She wondered if there was some easy way out of the play. Maybe she could invent a sudden demand by her mother for music lessons. "Dear Ms. Avery, Stephanie has to be able to play the harpsichord by June ... " She wouldn't be able to hide such a scheme from Arthur, but he could be silenced. Threats of near death usually worked. Or maybe there was such a thing as an allergy to stage-dust? She narrowed her eyes and tried to feel scratchy.

"So," Ms. Avery was saying, "that takes care of the practical details. I'll be working out a rehearsal schedule as soon as I can, and I'll post a copy outside the office. It will be up to you to know when you're supposed to show up. Right now, I'd like to start a read-through. We don't have time to get all the way through the play, but we can start. Scripts out, everyone, and Lucky," she looked at Joey, "you have the opening line."

"All right!" Joey said enthusiastically. "Lucky leads the way!"

And as quickly as that, everyone there found themselves flipped out of their private reveries and swimming in the uncharted waters of *Blood and Moonlight*.

CHAPTER 9

As LD headed home through the winter twilight, she was blissfully absorbed in the thought of the work that lay ahead of her. In one pocket she carried a book Mr. Raditch had given her, *Building for the Stage*. In her binder was a copy of the script, and the beginnings of a scene-by-scene breakdown. When the planning and designing were complete, LD thought with great satisfaction, it would be up to her to build it all.

When she walked into the garage, she saw her father deep in conversation with his assistant, Jeff.

" . . . don't want her to be alone when I'm gone," her father was saying seriously. "You understand." The words hit LD like a boot to the pit of the stomach.

"Sure, Mr. D, I can see that. But I can't
— " Jeff stopped when he saw LD standing
white-faced in the shadows.

"LD," her father said when he saw her.
"Hello." He looked at his watch. "It's late.
Did you stop somewhere?"

"I had a meeting," she said. "About the
school play." Her voice sounded flat and distant to her, but she was remotely surprised
that she could speak at all.

Her father's face lit up. "You're going to
be in a play?" he said. "That's fantastic."

Jeff grinned. "Hey, LD, you're going to be
an actress? That's great. How about that,
Mr. D? Meryl Streep the second, hey?"

LD couldn't believe their reaction—trying
to cover up what they had been talking
about, and acting as if the dumb play was
important. She tightened her lips. "I'm not
going to be an actress, okay? I'm not going
to be in the play, I'm just going to work on
it. I'm going to build the sets, and it's going
to take a lot of time."

Frank Delacorte's face fell. "Well," he
said, groping for something to say, "that's
very nice, LD. That's — "

"You don't think it's nice at all," LD said
bluntly. "You wish I was a fluffed-up Cin-
derella or something! A little doll in a satin
dress! Well, I'm not! You said you want me
to be able to take care of myself, and so
that's what I'm doing. I don't care what you
do. I've got a life of my own, and I like to

make things! And at least I'm honest!!!" And then she stormed out of the garage into the kitchen, where she promptly tripped on a chair leg, flung out an arm to catch her balance, and sent a teacup crashing into the sink.

When her father came in from closing up the garage for the night, he found the fragments of the cup still in the sink, and no sign of LD. He walked quietly to her bedroom door, heard music coming from her old radio, and went back to the kitchen without saying anything. Then he began to fish the bits of china out of the sink, and throw them in the garbage.

Frank Delacorte was halfway through a plateful of spaghetti when LD walked into the kitchen two hours later. "Hungry?" he asked. "Pull up a chair."

LD saw that he had set a place for her. "Thanks." As she slid into her chair, she couldn't help glancing at the sink, but the remains of the cup had disappeared. She began helping herself.

When her plate was full, and she was about to start, she looked up at her father and said, "Dad?"

Mr. Delacorte had been working steadily on his plate, carefully ignoring his daughter. Now he looked up. "Yes, LD?"

"I'm sorry."

"Never mind," he said. "I think I understand."

"It's just that you've been acting funny lately," she said, "and I don't know what it means."

He made a wry smile. "You think *I've* been acting funny?"

"You mean . . . I have?" LD said in surprise. "What have I been doing?"

"Someday," he said, "you'll have a daughter of your own, and you'll find out."

"What does that mean?"

"It's too hard to explain," he said. "You have to be a hundred years old, like all parents, to understand. But never mind. I'm just glad you're working on the play. It will give me something to look forward to — a sort of consolation prize." Now that you're here, there's something I need to talk to you about."

LD had been covering her spaghetti with a uniform quarter inch of Parmesan cheese. Now she stopped. *This is it,* LD thought. *He's going to tell me he's got two months to live.* She wanted to get up and run to her room, but she couldn't move. She couldn't take her eyes from his face.

"When is the play, exactly?"

"The play? The last week in February. Why?"

"Well, I want to go, of course. And now I'll be here for it."

She felt her insides turn to cold Jello. "What do you mean, now? Why wouldn't you be here?" She put the cheese down and looked at him in alarm. "Are you, I mean, is it — is it your ... " She couldn't bring herself to say it.

"Is it my heart? No, no, for heaven's sake, LD, it's nothing like that. You've got to forget about my health. Didn't I tell you I'm as strong as an ox? No, I thought I was going away on a trip."

LD looked at him in wordless astonishment. She couldn't remember him ever going anywhere, except across town to pick up parts. He might as well have told her he had decided to grow feathers. "A trip where?" she said finally.

"To Corsica. I wanted to go and visit our village."

Slowly the panic that had gripped her was melting away, but LD's mind still whirled in confusion. "Our village?" she said slowly. "But you were never even there. Grandma and Grampa had just got married when they left and came here."

"That's why I wanted to go there," he said. "We have lots of cousins there, and people who remember my father and mother. I — well, I told you my health is good now, but being in the hospital made me think about things like this. Family. Tradition. It's important."

LD continued to stare. All the alarm signals of the past week fell into place — the photograph albums, the — "That day you were dressed up," she said suddenly. "Was that — ?"

"I was going to the travel agent. You have to book these tickets in advance, you know, or it costs a lot more."

LD became aware that her mouth was slightly drier than the Sahara. She swallowed convulsively and began to think. "What about me?"

"I thought about taking you with me," he replied, "but I couldn't afford it. And you shouldn't be out of school so long."

"How long are you going for?" she asked.

He smiled sadly. "I told you, I can't go. I planned to go for six weeks. I would leave in — " He squinted at the calendar. " — ten days or so. And I'd be gone until the beginning of March."

"That's a long time!"

"Well, if I fly now, it's cheap, and in March is Great-uncle Jerome's hundredth birthday. I'd want to stay for that."

"But, then, why aren't you going?" LD felt the gears begin to grind in her mind. He was talking about a holiday! A rest! Something good for him, for a change!

"I thought I could get Jeff to stay here while I was gone, to keep an eye on you, but he says it won't work."

LD remembered the overheard conversation a few hours earlier. "Why not?"

"He's got his new girlfriend. I think

66

they're going to get a place together. But anyway, he's more interested in spending time with her, and I don't blame him."

"Then . . . I could stay here on my own." The idea was attractive and alarming at the same time. If she got thirty or forty dozen eggs and a couple of gallons of hot sauce, that should take care of the food — but it would be so lonely.

"I don't think so." As she began to react, he added hastily, "It isn't that you couldn't do it, LD. It's just that I want someone around to help you if you need it. So, since Jeff can't stay here, I'll have to phone tomorrow and cancel my ticket. I can go another time."

"No! Don't do that! I can go and stay with someone."

"Who?"

LD thought fast. "Voula," she said. "Voula's always asking me to stay over. Sure, she'd let me stay there while you were gone."

He looked at her doubtfully. "But what about her parents?"

"They wouldn't mind," LD bluffed. "I get along with her dad great. And he's used to girls."

"Well, that's something. Otherwise, the shock might kill him! I wouldn't want to have that on my conscience."

"So, it's okay? You won't cancel your trip?"

"Well, not if you can stay with Voula. But

67

if I have to, I can go another time."

But as she finally dug into her spaghetti, LD made a firm promise to herself that her father would visit Corsica. It wasn't often he showed signs of taking care of himself, and she thought he should be encouraged. And as for convincing Voula and her parents that she would make an ideal house guest for six whole weeks, well . . . she would build that bridge when she came to it.

CHAPTER 10

Susie stood in the middle of the stage, with a pen tucked behind her ear. On her shirt was a large button that read, "Ask ME. (If I don't know the answer, I'll make one up.)" She was trying to organize the crew and rehearsal schedules.

Just then LD came on stage. "Hi, LD," Susie said. "Technical crew in the carpentry shop in five minutes, right?"

"Uh, yeah." She raised a clenched fist and tried to sound like a foreman. "Right! Prepare to sweat!"

Turning toward the shop, LD was nearly trampled by Joey and Wheels. "So you want to be called Lucky," Wheels was saying. "Fine. But I don't want to be called Eddy, all right?"

"But, Whee — I mean, Eddy, my man, it's part of being an actor. We have to identify with our parts! Besides, it doesn't work if you don't do it, too."

LD watched them disappear into the green room, and then saw Voula headed in the same direction. At the sight of her, LD gathered her courage. She had worried all day about asking Voula if she could stay with her. She knew her father didn't want her to be alone while he was away, and she understood. She had seen enough scary television to know that for every girl home alone quietly eating pizza there were three or four dangerous criminals prowling in the hedges. But at the same time, she couldn't forget the way Voula's father had met her at the door last week. LD doubted he approved of her.

But if she didn't have somewhere to stay, her father would cancel his trip, and she didn't want that. What could be better for him than a rest in a warm climate?

"Voula," she said, "can I talk to you?"

"Oh, hi, LD," Voula said. "What is it?"

Briefly LD explained about her father's trip and her need to stay somewhere while he was away.

Voula listened seriously, and then said, "Oh, LD, I wish you could stay with us. But my grandmother is coming to visit next week and we won't have any room. Even if we did," she added, "I don't think you would want to. She's awfully strict about stuff. She thinks girls should wear long-sleeved dresses. She'd even dress me up in black, if she could!"

Voula continued to talk about her grandmother, but LD was wondering what she was going to do about a place to stay. She got along with kids at school, but she wasn't really close to anyone. No one shared her love of machines, and she felt shy and out of place outside of the garage. So when she looked at the students around her, there wasn't anyone who seemed a likely candidate.

" ... I'm really sorry, LD," Voula was saying. "Maybe when she's gone, you could come some weekend and sleep over. But that won't be until April. Grandma believes in long visits!"

"Uh, sure," LD said. "That would be great, Voula. Thanks ... " What was she going to do?

Before the technical meeting got under way, LD walked around the shop, taking stock. She felt safe in the shop, and the worry about a place to stay faded as she peered in corners and cupboards. There were a few good machine tools, and a power stapler that might work, but the hand tools were a mess. She found a screwdriver that looked like it had been used in hand to hand combat with megadroids, and the only hammer had a head that fell off when she picked it up. In one cupboard, among paint cans and petri-fied brushes, she found a blaze orange hard hat with a decal of a gorilla on the front. She pulled it out and replaced her blue garage cap with it.

"It's you," said Heather, who had been sitting at the table waiting for the meeting to start. "Especially the gorilla."

LD grinned and sat down at the table. "I'm going ape over the stage," she said.

"Don't monkey with us, LD!" Snake said.

Spike groaned. "You guys are terrible. Let's start, okay?"

Just then, Yick came in and took the last chair. "Okay," LD said. "Let's see how far we've got. You go first, Spike."

"Well," Spike said, laying a number of sketches on the table, "this is how we think the sets should look." She and Annie had been working together, studying interiors. "We went over the script pretty carefully, and I think we've got everything we need. We don't need much furniture. In fact, it's better if we don't have any. We can get old packing cases to sit on, and for a table. And a mattress, and rags for curtains. And Annie says the walls should be plaster, broken in places, so that you can see the lath inside. We can stuff a dead rat in there to make it really scuzzy."

"You can't stuff a rat in there," LD said, "even if we had one. The walls will be stretched canvas."

Spike looked startled for a moment. "Uh, yeah. Right. Well, we can paint a rat on the wall, then."

"Okay, that's the Wark apartment," LD said. "What about the other sets?"

One by one they went through the scenes. Everyone agreed that the sketches looked good. "But what are we going to do about changing scenes?" asked LD.

"We were hoping you would tell us," Spike said.

"Maybe we could cut a couple of the scenes out," Yick said. "Like the ghost scene."

"That's our last resort," said Snake. "We shouldn't change the play unless we have to."

"I know!" Spike said. "We have all the scenes onstage at once."

"How?" asked Snake.

"Just like a doll's house, when you open it up," Spike explained. "But we only turn the lights on in one part at a time." She drew a quick sketch of a rectangle divided in five parts. "Suppose this is the stage, and down here is the Wark apartment. Beside it could be the hang-out in the basement. Up here might be the schoolyard, and so on."

Snake looked at her sketch doubtfully. "All the actors would be squished together in one little room," he said, "and four-fifths of the stage would be dark at any one time."

"I suppose," Spike said, "but couldn't we —"

"No," LD said bluntly, cutting her off. "It won't work." Spike looked at her in hurt surprise, but LD was looking around the table to see if anyone else had an idea. Nobody said anything.

Suddenly LD sat up straight. "I know how we can do it," she declared. "We can build a turntable."

Everyone looked at her blankly. "A big turntable, the size of the stage," she explained. "I read about it in this book." She fished Mr. Raditch's book out of her pocket as evidence. "Then we divide the turntable into segments, and each segment is a different setting."

There was a short silence while everyone digested this. Then Snake said, "Okay. I understand that each scene is like a piece of the pie. But we need five scenes, and if you divide the turntable circle into five segments, then each segment is going to be sort of skinny."

"Not to mention," Spike said, "that you would be able to see some of the other sections when you weren't supposed to. It's not that much better than my idea, if you ask me."

LD's face fell. She hadn't thought as far as this.

Then Snake was struck by an inspiration of his own.

"The turntable will work," he said, "if we divide it into three sections."

"But we need five," Spike protested.

"No problem." Snake picked up a pen and drew a circle, then divided it into three wedges. "While one segment is facing the audience, the other two are out of sight, right? So we can change them. We have three blank areas, and we just move things on and off as we need them. Put a mattress and some packing cases on, and it's the Wark place. Stick a basketball hoop and some old garbage on it, and it becomes the schoolyard." He looked around the table. "What do you think?"

"Wouldn't it be a lot of work to build something like that?" Heather asked.

"I could do it," LD said. "I even know where I could get stuff for the hub. Let's try."

There were still doubtful looks around the table. "Listen, if I'm in charge," LD said, her voice rising, "then it's up to me, and I say we're going to do it. So that settles it." There was stunned silence at this undemocratic move, but LD ignored it. "Yick, what about the special effects?"

"I know where I can get a flashing light," Yick said, "and the school has a starter's pistol. I haven't found a siren yet."

LD made notes. "What about the ghost?"

Yick blinked nervously. "I haven't . . . um . . . thought of anything. Yet."

"Well, you'd better," LD said flatly, "or this play will look like broomhead city. Oh,

75

and did you notice that the ghost has stab wounds in the back?"

Yick licked his lips. "S-stab wounds? Really?"

"Mmm," said Heather. "Lots of blood! Let me know if you need any help, Yick."

"Sure," Yick said. "Blood. Ha-ha. Of course. . . . "

"Hey, LD, wait up!" Still trying to juggle his books into a manageable armful, Snake came hurrying along the street after the solitary, retreating figure. The meeting had broken up a few moments before, and everyone had scattered quickly.

"Hi," said LD, wondering what he wanted. She and Snake had probably exchanged all of six words up until now.

"That was a great idea," Snake said, starting to walk along with her. "The turntable."

"Oh," LD said. "I read it in that book."

"Yeah, but you thought of it for us," he persisted. "I like it. It's going to look great. But how are you going to build it?"

LD looked at him with surprise and a flicker of suspicion. "Well, it's got to turn smoothly," she said, "so I figure we can use a car wheel on its side as the hub, with the axle and bearings anchored somehow, and then bolt the platform to the wheel. That should do it."

Snake looked at her for a moment, thinking. LD noticed that he had light copper-colored hair that broke in soft waves around the nape of his neck. "Yeah," he said slowly, "but the platform will be heavy, especially with actors and furniture on it. It might not work like that."

"Those bearings will take it," LD declared. "They're built to take a lot of lateral force on turns, you know. But we could always go to something bigger, like a truck wheel. I could get one of those from the garage, I think."

"No," Snake said, "that's not what I mean. I mean the platform will droop at the edges and stick, unless you make it really stiff. How are you going to do that?"

"Well, if you don't like the idea, why don't you just say so? Why didn't you say so in the meeting?" LD flared.

"What are you talking about?" Snake said. "I told you it's a great idea. I'm just thinking about the problems, that's all."

"Well, the problems with the turntable are my problems. You think about the problems with lights and sound."

Snake gave her a strange look. "Sure," he said. "Anything you say. See you later, boss." And he turned and crossed the street, leaving her to walk on alone.

CHAPTER 11

The first full rehearsal started out in the green room.

"Why is it called green?" asked Arthur, looking around at the drab yellow walls.

"Because," Susie said with a grin, "you go green waiting for your turn to go on. This is where you wait, you know. Sometimes people have gone crazy from the strain."

"Oh, sure," Erica said. "Tell us another one."

"It's true," Susie said. "My brother told me about this play they did at the university, and there was this one actress who was really nervous, waiting in the green room. And she didn't go on until the last act or something, so she had a really long wait. And then she missed her cue. So they went to the green room to see what had happened to her, and they found her, lying flat on her back, with her eyes wide open, chewing on — "

Just then, Ms. Avery hurried in carrying an armload of books and papers, threw herself into a battered armchair beside Susie, and said, "Did I make it?"

Susie checked her watch. "Twelve seconds early," she said.

"Thank goodness!" said Ms. Avery. "I hope everyone else is here." Her eyes swept around the room, taking in each face. "Yes," she said at last. "Then let's get down to business."

From the corner of the room where Joey was sitting with Wheels and Alex, a small voice sang, "There's no business like show business . . . "

"The first piece of business," Ms. Avery said, "is this. As long as we are in rehearsal, I expect you all to behave like professionals. In plain words, that means keeping a lid on it until it's your turn. Anyone who can't control him or herself will be out of here, and I mean now. There is no one who can't be replaced if he or she doesn't know how to cooperate." She paused and looked around the room again. "Do I make myself clear?"

A few heads nodded. A few others glanced over at Joey, but he showed no sign he thought the speech might be directed at him.

"Good," said Ms. Avery. "Today I want to move onto the stage, show you some warm-up exercises, and get you familiar with the space. Then we'll split into two groups, one with me and one with Susie, and we'll work through a couple of scenes. Any questions? No? Let's go, then. Bring your scripts."

As they filed through the door toward the stage, Stephanie found herself beside Joey. "Way to go, Joey," she said. "Real mature."

"It wasn't me!" Joey protested.

"Oh, right. I forgot — you're too sophisticated. Only a bag-brain juvenile would interrupt a rehearsal."

"Hey," Joey said to no one in particular as Steph moved away into the gloom of the wings, "it's a bum rap. Lucky was framed, right?"

But no one who heard him believed it.

" . . . Then, after you've done a physical warm-up, you have to warm up your voice," Ms. Avery said. "There are lots of ways of doing this, but I know one that works really well, and will probably make you relax, too, because you end up laughing so much. It's simple. You count up to fifteen like this: one, one two, one two three, one two three four, and so on. But you have to keep your tongue stuck out as far as you can all the time. Let's see you try it."

The stage filled with laughter as the students stuck out their tongues and tried to count.

"Wunh, wunh 'oo, wunh 'oo hwhee . . . "
Erica looked at Stephanie and cracked up.
"You're crossing your eyes!" she said.

Stephanie crossed her eyes even more, and
the two fell apart in giggles.

"First one to fifteen wins," called Ms.
Avery, "but say it as clearly as you can."

Arthur frowned in serious concentration
as he tried to enunciate clearly with most of
his tongue outside his mouth.

When at last they had finished, Ms. Avery
said, "Everything feels a lot looser, now,
doesn't it? All right. Now the last part of
the warm-up you can't really do right now,
because we're just getting started, but it is
to get into character. Being an actor means
more than just standing in the right spot
and saying the right lines. It means *becoming* the character you are playing. Forget
about Lucy or Steph or Wheels, and become
Carmen or Mrs. Wark or Eddy. It's a complete transformation. But we are just starting to form our characters. That part of the
warm-up will be easier after you have
learned your lines. Which I hope you can
have done by the end of the month, please.
Okay, I want the people in Act Two, Scene
One to go with Susie to the green room, and
the rest of us will work here. Read through
as much as you can, and try to *be* your
character . . . "

CHAPTER 12

Arthur waited while Yick opened his locker to get his coat. "I wish I knew what it was like to be poor," he said. "It will be impossible to understand this play without knowing real poverty."

Yick gave him a wordless glance and pulled open the locker door. Then he stiffened. "Hey!" he said. "Did you do this?"

"Do what?" Arthur peered over Yick's shoulder. At the bottom of his locker, perched on the layers of books, lunch bags, defunct running shoes, notes from assorted classes and other debris, there was a stick of dynamite. Looking more closely, he saw it was a cardboard tube from a roll of paper towels, painted red. From one end ran a short rope fuse, the end of which was also painted red. Stencilled on the thing in big black letters was the word, "DANGER!"

Yick picked it up. "What's this doing here?" he demanded.

"I don't know," Arthur said. "I didn't put it there. Wasn't your locker locked?"

"Sure." Yick gestured with the lock he still held in his other hand. "I just opened it."

"Someone must know your combination, then. Or there's something really weird about your locker."

At that moment Mr. Raditch came down the hall. Seeing the stick of dynamite in Yick's hand, he gave him a curious look. "Taking the special effects a little seriously, aren't you, Yick?"

Yick opened his mouth to reply, but it seemed too difficult to explain. "Uh . . . yes, sir."

As they left the school, Yick said, "This is starting to worry me, Arthur. I guess I have to get another lock. Or set a trap of some kind. I could rig up a siren to go off when they open my locker. When I find a siren . . . " If it is a real person at all, he thought. Would the school let him have another locker if this one was haunted? He glanced quickly behind him, but the hallway appeared normal. Even so, he felt a prickle of alarm run down his back.

Outside, although the day was overcast, the air was mild, making the snowbanks slump softly. Yick and Arthur tramped along through the slush and across the occasional dry island of sidewalk. Arthur was still preoccupied with the idea of being poor.

"I mean," he said, "in the play, we're supposed to be *really* poor. Nothing to eat and stuff like that. We've never been that poor. Have you?"

Yick looked at him out of the corner of his eye for a moment, but didn't say anything.

"I thought of not eating for a day or two, but I don't think it's a good idea. It might worry my father. He feels responsible for me, I think."

Finally Yick said, "I don't know what the big deal is about being poor, Arthur. Lots of people have been poor. You should just talk to them."

Arthur vaguely remembered something Yick had once mentioned about his past. "Have you been poor?" he asked.

"Well . . . yeah. We were poor for a while."

"What was it like?"

Yick thought for a moment. "We didn't have anything."

"I know that! But what was it *like?*"

"Look," Yick said, "learning to think poor is your problem. My problem is special effects. I need to find gunshots, a police siren, and a ghost in moonlight, not to mention a new lock for my locker." They had arrived at the Degrassi Grocery, where their ways parted.

"Well," Arthur said, "I was just trying to find out."

"Yeah," Yick said. "Well, I'll see what I can remember. I was sort of little when we were really poor. If I think of anything, I'll tell you. See you tomorrow."

"Yeah," Arthur said. "Tomorrow." But instead of turning for home, he watched Yick walk away for a moment and then went into the grocery. "Excuse me," he said, "where do you keep your dog food?"

Yick walked home deep in thought. He was having difficulty thinking of a suitable ghost, but it wasn't because he didn't believe in them. It was because he knew too much about ghosts. One of his earliest memories, long before his family had come to this country, was of hearing the story of the ghost at the well in the next street over from their house. In the end, the well had been abandoned because no one wanted to go there, even in daylight. And everyone in the family knew the story of his aunt, who had been practically driven crazy by uncanny shrieks in the night. It had taken many visits from the local priest and about a ton of incense before the disturbances had ended.

If you made an imaginary ghost, Yick thought, might that not be a sign inviting *real* ghosts to come around? It was an unsettling thought. He was sure you could summon ghosts. After all, his grandfather had once told him how, according to tradition, ghosts and evil spirits could be chased away with . . .

A smile spread across Yick's face as the beginning of a plan settled comfortably in his mind.

A lump of snow had fallen onto the sidewalk ahead of him. In perfect soccer form, Yick brought his foot back and sent the lump spraying into oblivion. Yes, the plan might work . . .

By the time Arthur got home, the round bulge in his pocket was making him acutely self-conscious. He had the impression that every person on the street had been able to identify the contents of his pocket, and to know exactly why he was carrying a can of Bowser brand dog food.

His father wasn't home yet, which was fortunate. Somehow, Arthur thought that the experiment he was about to try might upset him.

He put the can of dog food on the counter and took out a can opener. "Beef stew flavor — real meaty taste," said the label. There was a cartoon of a dog licking its lips with a bright-red, foot-long tongue.

Reluctantly, Arthur opened the can and lifted off the sharp-rimmed silver disk. The brown, gelatinous mass in the can quivered a little as he looked at it. Slowly he took a spoon out of the drawer, and even more slowly poked it into the dog food. As he lifted a spoonful out of the can, the smell hit him. It smelled like beef stew, all right. But what was in it — really? He got out a bowl and scraped the contents of the can into it, even though he figured that really poor people wouldn't have bowls, or maybe even spoons. But they would have to have can openers, wouldn't they? If not, how would they get at the dogfood?

After he had stood for a long time, staring at the mess in the bowl, he thought he remembered that he was supposed to stop at his mom's place tonight to pick up some mail that had come for his dad. Actually, his mom had said he could get it anytime, but it might be important. He could try the dog food later. He fished out an empty margarine tub from the cupboard, dumped the dog food in it, and put it in the fridge. Then he threw the can in the garbage, put away the opener, and went out. He felt a lot lighter than he had. Maybe there was something to those acting exercises, after all.

Erica, Heather, Lucy and Stephanie were in a booth at the malt shop, steadily demolishing a plate of fries. Every so often Erica would vary her diet by fishing an ice cube from her empty glass, and crunching it noisily between her teeth.

"How can you do that?" demanded Stephanie, after the fifth chunk of ice had vanished this way. "It makes my teeth practically fall out of my head every time you do it."

"I like it," Erica said.

"But doesn't it hurt your teeth?"

Eric popped another cube in her mouth, and said around it, "Oh, come on, mother."

"What do you mean, 'mother'?" asked Stephanie.

"Well, you are. That's your part in the play, and that's what you sound like now."

"I do not," she said, hurt. "And anyway, I'm not *your* mother. I'm Lucy's mother."

Lucy gave her a big grin. "Hey, Mom, can I have the car tonight for a real heavy date?" Steph laughed weakly. She didn't want to be Lucy's mother, either.

"There's something I don't understand," Heather said. "Lucy, you're supposed to be Steph's daughter, but you don't look at all alike. I mean, for one thing, you're black."

"Well," Lucy said, looking wide-eyed and innocent, "my old man, *Mister* Wark, ran off when I was just a baby, but I *suspect* that *he* was black."

"See?" Erica said to her sister.

"Oh, yeah, right," Heather said, and tapped her forehead. "Sometimes it takes me a while."

Lucy leaned forward and gripped Heather's arm. "You've got no idea," she said seriously, "what it was like, growing up in the project with no father, and my mother trying to raise three kids on welfare and odd jobs. I been looking after the little ones since I was six!"

Heather laughed nervously and looked at the others for support.

"We have to do that all the time," explained Erica. "It's called Developing our Characters. Like moth — " she caught sight of the ominous look on Stephanie's face and stopped, " — like Angel's passion for Eddy," she said, and turned to look at Wheels who was sitting two booths away with Joey and Alex. She continued to stare until Wheels looked her way, and then she quickly turned back to her own table. "It worked," she laughed.

"What are you doing?" Stephanie asked.

"Developing my character," Erica said, and she casually looked over her shoulder again until Alex noticed her and nudged Wheels. When Wheels looked up, she turned quickly away again. "It works every time," she said.

Stephanie didn't laugh. She was facing the booth where the three boys sat, and she saw they were now staring openly at Erica. "Real grown up," she said drily. "I mean, that's *totally* sophisticated, Erica."

"It's just an assignment," she said, taking

a noisy slurp of her Coke. "Wheels and I might have to do some serious homework to get it right, though." Very casually, she glanced out the window, and then just happened to look behind her . . .

Stephanie walked home through a tossing sea of emotion. She had been so concerned about the role of Carmen—the role of Eddy's girlfriend, given to Lucy instead of herself — that she had forgotten about Carmen's rival, Angel. Now Erica was fixing her sights on Wheels, and Steph couldn't tell if it was just pretend, to try and build up her "character," or if it was meant to be real. The only thing she was sure of was that she hated this play, and she wished it had never even been thought of.

When she got home, she was surprised to find her brother sitting in front of the television, eating chocolate chip cookies. "What are you doing here?" she said. "This isn't your weekend to visit."

"I came over to pick up the mail that came for Dad," Arthur said, "but I can't find it."

"Have you got socks for brains, or what?" she demanded. "You took it to him a week ago."

"I did?" A vague memory bobbed to the surface of Arthur's mind. "Oh, yeah — I guess I did."

"And you better get back there now," Stephanie ordered. "You're going to be late for dinner."

"Right," said Arthur. "I'm on my way. Uh . . . is anything wrong?"

"Why?"

"You seem unusually mad at me today," he said. "More than average hostile."

"Well, it's nothing *you'd* understand, anyway." And she marched determinedly upstairs. A little brother — who was sometimes her son, if you could believe it — was the last thing she wanted to deal with right now.

When Arthur got home, he found his father in the kitchen, peering at the hockey scores in the sports section, and absently spooning food into his mouth. "Hi, son," he said. "Thanks for taking care of dinner."

Arthur froze. "What do you mean?"

"I found that stew you made. I didn't know you could cook like that. Grab a plate. I saved some for you."

Arthur felt his throat clamp shut all on its own, with iron determination. "I don't think I'm very hungry right now. Maybe later."

"Suit yourself," his father said, "but you're missing one first class meal!" And he scooped up another mouthful of Bowser brand dog food. "You'll have to give me your recipe."

"Uh . . . no. I can't do that," Arthur said,

trying desperately to think of a good reason why not. "I just can't."

His father glanced up from the paper. "Oh, I get it. Trade secrets. Well, just as long as you promise to make it again sometime!"

CHAPTER 13

When Lucy got home, the house was, as usual, in darkness. Dropping her books on the sofa, she went to the phone machine and ran it back. Then she left it to play while she stuck her head in the fridge. After two no-message calls, her mother's voice come out of the black box.

"Hi, sweetie. See what you can find in the fridge. I think there's some tortellini with pesto you could heat up. I'll be home about seven, and then we have to go and see the counsellor. Daddy will meet us there. Love ya." Then, immediately, her mother was on the line again in the next message. "Hi, it's me. If you don't find anything to eat, maybe we can go out after the counselling for a pizza. Gotta go, sweetheart. Bye . . . "

After the machine had run on for another five minutes without revealing further news, Lucy turned it off. She had found the tortellini, but she wasn't very hungry. Maybe soup and toast . . .

Lucy stared bleakly around the silent white kitchen, waiting for water to boil. When her soup was ready, she sat down with it at the kitchen table, and pulled out her copy of the script. As she looked at her first speech, the image of the cavernous stage floated before her eyes. In the middle of the stage stood Wheels. Erica was right. He was kind of cute. Maybe she should phone him? But he would be eating dinner now, and afterward she had to go out. Besides, she knew that Steph still had eyes for him, and it wasn't her style to move in like that. Of course, if Wheels noticed *her*, well, that was a different matter.

Pushing her soup aside, she set to work on her lines. But she had only read through half a page when the phone rang. Eagerly, she grabbed the receiver. "Hello?"

"Carmen, baby. Is that you?" said a voice.

"Who is this?"

"This is your lucky day, Carmen. It's your old pal Lucky."

"Joey?"

"You got it. Joey P. Jeremiah. P for Primo Performance, if you know what I mean. Wanna put on a show with me?"

"What are you talking about?"

"The stage, baby, the stage. How about you and me going over some lines tonight?"

"You and me?" Lucy said. "We don't have any lines, do we? I mean together."

"Sure we do. What about Act Two, Scene Five?"

Lucy flipped through her script. "It's really short," she said. "Two lines each."

"It's a start," said Joey. "And I'm great at improvs. Who knows what could happen."

"Joey," Lucy said, "is this a come-on? Are you asking me for a date or something?"

There was a moment's silence, and then in an altered voice Joey said, "I just thought it would be nice if we worked on the play together, that's all."

"Well, that's sweet, but there's hardly anything for us to work *on*," Lucy said, "and anyway, I can't tonight. I've got to go out in a little while."

"Okay," Joey said. "Some other time. See you at school."

"Sure," Lucy said. "Bye." As she hung up the phone, she sighed. Why didn't Wheels make her an offer like that?

While they washed the dishes, LD's father said, "So, did you ask Voula?"

LD, her hands hidden under a cloud of detergent foam, felt her knees go funny. She began to scrub vigorously at a plate that was already clean. "Ah, sure . . . "

95

"Yes?" her father said. "And?"

"She thinks it will be all right. She had to ask her parents."

Her father paused to polish a glass, and then said, "You don't want to stay with her, do you?"

"What? No, it's okay. I want to."

He put the glass away and took another from the draining rack. "Maybe I shouldn't go . . . "

LD turned from the sink. "You have to!" she said in alarm. "You have to go!"

"Is it that hard to put up with me?" he asked. "Just teasing," he said before she could reply. "I know you want me to go. But maybe it isn't the right time. Maybe I could go later."

LD faced him squarely. "Look, you're going, all right? You've got the tickets and everything. You have to. What about Uncle Jerome's birthday?"

He smiled. "Okay, LD. You're the boss." When she relaxed, he added, "And if I don't go, I can always hole up in a hotel here and read books about Corsica!"

"What?"

"I'll get Uncle Jerome to send you a post card from me. 'Ma chère Lorraine — ' "

"Don't you dare! Don't even think of it!"

Laughing, he dodged away from her wet dishcloth.

Later, LD sat in her room and tried to put thoughts of her father and his trip out of her mind. She had to design the stiffest turntable ever, and make it out of shoeboxes and string. She pulled a pad of paper toward her and began to sketch ideas.

The din filling the basement was loud enough to shake paint off the walls, but it didn't matter. Wheels' parents would be out for another hour at least. Wheels gyrated and slapped his bass as though it were a wild animal fighting back. Beside him, Snake enthusiastically throttled his guitar, while Joey attacked the synthesizer keyboard like a madman. All three of them were howling the lyrics to their latest song, 'I Don't Want to be a Porcupine with Anyone Else But You, Baby.'

Oh, I'm a great big rodent!
Yeah, that's me!
Full of sharp quills!
Like to climb a tree!

They were revving up for the final chorus, getting even louder, if that was possible.

Do you like my spines?
Do you like my tree?
Do you want to sit on a branch with me?
Hey I don't wanna be
No, no, I just can't be,
No, I don't want to be
A porcupi-yi-yi-yi-yiyi-yine
With anyone! else!! but!! you!!! Baby!!!!!!

The finale was a freeform minute-long collision of riffs, slaps and chords, as they each tried to be the instrument playing the final notes.

When the walls had stopped ringing, they looked at each other and nodded. "Not bad," said Snake. "Could be a hit."

"Not bad?" said Joey. "Are you kidding? This could revolutionize the pop music industry. No one is doing music like this, man. No one."

Wheels slipped the bass strap from around his neck. "You guys want something to drink?"

"Hey, sure," said Snake.

"Right," Joey said, putting on his dark glasses. "Let's take five. Or six even. Irrigate our tonsils."

They trooped upstairs to the kitchen, emptied the refrigerator of its last three cans of pop, and then, because they felt less like a band above ground, went back down to the cool, musty gloom of the basement.

"It's a real shame," Joey said, "they can't use a song like Porcupine in the play."

"Doesn't really fit in, though," Snake said.

Wheels looked at Joey. "Have you started working on your character?"

"My character? Sure, man, I got Lucky all figured out. He's a cool dude."

"A cool dude?" Wheels said. "Are you

kidding? He's a jerk. I don't see how you can live with yourself, playing Lucky."

"What do you mean? He's just misunderstood, man. Disadvantaged. A victim of poverty."

"He's a junkie," Wheels declared, "and a creep. He's always stealing things, and causing trouble. He even tries to steal Eddy's girlfriend, and they're supposed to be friends."

"Just cause you get to play the hero," Joey said. "Mr. White Hat. Mr. Good Guy who gets the girl."

"That's not it, Joey," Wheels insisted. "Lucky is just slime, that's all. He was the guy that killed Sharkey the Stiff."

"He did not!"

"He did so! Read the play. It's in there, man, in black and white."

"Hey," Snake said, "cool out, you guys. It's only a play. How about this for a topic. Anybody noticed the change in Stephanie Kaye, class president?"

"Who hasn't?" said Wheels. "But does anyone know why?"

Joey shrugged. "Maybe she's trying to act like a mother."

"A mother!" Snake said incredulously. "Pretty hard to imagine Stephanie as your mother."

Wheels shook his head. "She was different

from the start of term. Before we got into the play."

Snake grinned. "Does it make you change your mind about her, Wheels?"

"Nah, not really. She's cute, all right, but I don't know if I can take any more disaster. We just don't work out." He stared reflectively at the frets of his bass. "Actually, I've been sort of looking at Lucy lately ... "

"Yeah?" said Snake. "Lucy?"

"Well ... she's neat ... and we do have a lot of heavy scenes to work through, if you know what I mean ... " Wheels was suddenly aware of Joey watching him closely. "Hey," he said briskly, looking at his watch, "we don't have a lot of time before my folks come home. Why don't we run through 'Worms of Fire'?"

"Sure," Snake said, and picked up his guitar. "One of my faves."

But Joey said, "That song stinks."

Wheels was startled. "What? You never said so before."

"It just needs work," Snake said. "We just need to rehearse it more."

"It just needs to be buried," Joey said bluntly. He slid off his stool and stood up. "I gotta do some stuff. I'll see you guys later."

"Yeah, sure," Wheels said, but Joey was already on his way up the stairs. After he had gone, Wheels looked at Snake, completely baffled. "Was it something we said?"

"I don't know," Snake replied. "Maybe the pop ate through to his brain and short-circuited it."

"Uh, yeah, maybe," Wheels said. But he had the uneasy feeling there was more to Joey's outburst than a can of pop.

CHAPTER 14

A banner hung across one end of the hall-way: "Blood and Moonlight — Feb 25–28, Tickets coming soon . . . " And the intercom was saying, " . . . Students are reminded that rats, stuffed or otherwise, are *not* required for the play. However, donations of old clothes will be gratefully accepted by the wardrobe department . . . "

Lucy stared into her locker, where a page of her script was hanging from the top shelf. "Eddy," she read, "I been waiting for some-one for a long time . . . " She closed her eyes and repeated it. "I been waiting for someone for a long time. I been *waiting* for someone for a *long* time . . . I been waiting for *someone* . . . " She heard a sound beside her and opened her eyes to see LD at her locker.

"Hi," LD said. "Wouldn't it be easier to do that with Eddy?"

"Maybe," Lucy said. "Except that Wheels has been acting like a spooked rabbit around me."

"Really?"

"You haven't seen him in rehearsals. He stands way far away from me, and if Ms. Avery makes him get closer, he just freezes up!"

"Well," said LD, "why don't you thaw him out?"

Lucy smiled, and began to get her books ready for class. "I've thought of it," she said.

"Then what are you waiting for?"

"Well, for one thing," Lucy said, "it might make things worse. Maybe he really is scared of me. If he is, and I try to warm him up, he won't even come out on stage with me. And — I don't know ... " She looked down the hall to where Stephanie was talking to Erica and Heather.

LD followed her glance, and said, "Stephanie? But she's not going out with Wheels."

"No. But she'd like to. And it would make her feel bad ... "

"Hi, LD. Hi, Lucy." It was Voula. Since her grandmother had come to stay she had been dressing more conservatively than ever, usually arriving at school in shades of maroon and chocolate, and heavy, dark stockings. Today, however, her carefully brushed black hair was held in place by bright-yellow barrettes.

Lucy spotted them immediately. "Breaking out, Voula?" she asked.

Voula smiled self-consciously. "One small step for womankind . . . LD, have you found a place to stay yet?"

It was a question LD had been working overtime not to ask herself. Now a hunted look filled her eyes. "N-n-no. Not yet. I haven't asked anybody."

"Why do you need a place to stay?" asked Lucy.

"Her dad's going on a trip," Voula said. "For six weeks. But she can't stay at our place because of You Know Who."

"It's . . . ah . . . it's okay," LD said. "Don't worry about it. Just don't mention it to my dad, okay?"

"You mean — you're going to just stay at the garage by yourself?"

"What else can I do? He leaves tomorrow, but if I don't have a place to stay, he won't go. And he's *got* to go. It means a lot to him. So if you see him, just don't say anything, okay?"

"But — "

"I've got to go," LD said quickly, slamming her locker shut. "Work to do. I'll see you guys later."

Voula looked unhappily after LD as she walked away down the hall, but Lucy had a more thoughtful expression. "I have an idea," she said . . .

Meanwhile, with only a couple of minutes until class, Joey was just walking up the stairs to his second-floor locker. He ran into Wheels on the landing.

"Hi. How was your weekend?" Wheels said guardedly.

"Oh, smooth, real smooth. How about yours?"

"Fine." There was an awkward silence, and then Wheels said, "What were you so burned up about?"

Joey spread the fingers of both hands on his chest and said, "Burned up? Was I burned up?"

"Well, you left the band rehearsal pretty fast. It seemed like you were mad about something."

Joey opened his mouth to speak, hesitated, and then said, "Hey — it's cool, man. Under control, right? Just had to go do some stuff, that's all."

"Yeah? What about the axe job you did on 'Worms of Fire'?"

"Wheels, my man, you're taking it too hard! You did the lyrics, right? They're fine! I just meant Snake's music, that's all. He's a nice guy, but his chords are a little weird. Look, I've got to go ditch my coat. I'll see you in class."

105

He hurried up the stairs and through the doors. Watching him go, Wheels knew Joey was keeping something back. It didn't really matter to him what it was. What really bothered him was that Joey wouldn't tell him anything. Maybe they weren't as good friends as he had thought . . .

But Joey, firing his coat into his locker and grabbing the books he had neglected to take home over the weekend, could not have talked with anyone about what was chewing, with very sharp rat's teeth, at his insides. After the argument with Wheels about the true nature of Lucky, he had gone home and read the play carefully from beginning to end.

He was forced to admit that Wheels was right. Lucky was a weasel who caused trouble and used people — a lot.

Joey had thought that a guy named Lucky, who was head of the local gang, would be the hero. Because *he* was the head of *his* local gang — that's how he saw it, anyway — and he was no weasel . . . was he? After reading the play, Joey could not shake the feeling that he was being played for a sucker. Maybe he had got the part of Lucky because he was always getting in trouble, because people thought he was like Lucky. Maybe his friends saw him differently from what he thought. Maybe, after all, they weren't as good friends as he thought . . .

The bell rang, and Joey came to. He was alone in the hallway. Late again! If he really was the class creep, this wasn't going to help his image.

It was the start of another work session for the crew. Snake examined the framework for the turntable stage, flexing it gently.

"Hey, be careful with that, okay?" LD said.

"I won't hurt it." He walked around the platform that was slowly growing on the floor, studying the pattern of wooden supports.

Just then Shane came wandering into the shop. "Hi," he said, "what's happening here in sweat city?"

LD rounded on him. "You're late," she said. "Don't you know when you're supposed to be here?"

Shane looked at his watch. "So I'm a few minutes late," he said. "I was talking to Doris in the office."

"Talking to Doris won't build sets," LD said. "If you want to be part of this crew, be here on time."

Shane blinked at her in astonishment. "Yeah, sure," he said. "What do you want me to do?"

"See that pile of one-by-two?" She pointed to a stack of blond lumber against one wall.

"I need fourteen pieces, nine-foot-four each. Use the cut-off saw, and measure twice before you cut. The last time I don't think you measured at all."

Shane nodded warily, as though he had been given orders by a pit-bull terrier. "Anything you say, LD," he said. "You bet."

"And try to keep all your fingers," she added. If she had been less concerned with the job at hand, she might have noticed the large question mark floating in the air over Snake's head — but she didn't see it. Right now, she only wanted to see stage scenery, and lots of sawdust.

At that moment, Yick came in. He was wearing his coat and carrying a small paper bag. "You're late, too," LD said. "Don't any of you guys take this play seriously?"

Yick looked at her noncommittally. "I was out getting electrician's tape. We need it to hook up the police lights."

"Then you should have told me you were going," LD said. "We might have needed something else from the store, and you could have picked it up. You guys don't understand we have to work as a team, if we're going to get this done. And where is Spike?"

Nobody replied. Yick continued to watch her as if she were a cardboard box that ticked, but he didn't say anything. "Well, then," she said, "go hook up the lights. Do I have to tell you everything?"

A moment later, the cutoff saw began to howl and spit dust, so no one heard Yick, pawing through a drawer of tools, mutter, "If this is a team, I think I'd rather be playing for the other side . . . "

When LD got home, it was well after suppertime, but she was too tired to be hungry. She found her father sitting in his chair, wearing his reading glasses and peering at a map of Corsica.

"Hi!" LD said, trying to sound cheerful. "Picking out the best spots for your trip?"

He looked at her curiously over the tops of his glasses, but did not immediately say anything.

"You go tomorrow, right? Don't forget you promised to bring home a bottle of wine from our village."

He put the map down on the footstool. "LD. You know I can't go."

"What?"

"Tonight I phoned Mr. Grivogiannis. Voula's father. Just to see that everything is in order. He told me you can't stay there. He said you never even made plans to stay there."

LD stared at him wordlessly. "What were you going to do?" he asked. "Stay here alone?"

"I asked Voula," LD said. "I did. But she

said her grandmother was coming. I want you to go! I can look after myself. This trip is important! You've got to go!"

He shook his head. "No. I know you meant well. But I can't do that. So I'll go another time. If Uncle Jerome has lived this long, he'll last another year." Just then the phone rang. "I'll get it," he said. "You have something to eat."

But when he answered, it was for LD. Still numb, she put the phone to her ear and said tonelessly, "Hello?"

"LD? It's Lucy. Listen, I had to ask my mother about this first — that's why I didn't say anything this afternoon — but you can stay with us if you want. We've got lots of room."

"Really?" LD felt a grin starting to spread across her face, the first for a long time. "That's great, Lucy. But, uh, listen, you better talk to my dad about it, okay? He might not believe me right now . . . "

The next morning, before she left for school, LD said good-bye to her father. The two of them had stayed up late in the night, each packing. Now they stood in a kitchen full of suitcases, and there were only good-byes left. "I'm going to miss you," she said. "It seems funny to think you're going for a whole six weeks."

"The time will go before you know it," he

110

said. "You've got an important job. It will keep you busy." He gave her a quick hug. "Lorraine. I'll write you. Now, you better go — you'll be late for school." And it wasn't until she was outside that LD realized the look in his eyes was pride.

That night, LD moved in to Lucy's. "Here's a house key," Lucy said. "This is your bed, and you can have this half of the closet, and I emptied out these drawers for you — "

"I don't need much room," LD said. "I left a lot of stuff at home. I can get it if I need it."

"Oh, sure. Well, just make yourself at home. Actually, I have to go out now — I have some time scheduled with my dad at his office. We'll probably go to a movie, but we'll be home later. And my mom should be home *sometime*. You know what work is like . . . "

"Sure. It's okay. You go ahead. I'm sort of tired. I might just go to bed."

"Well," Lucy said, "suit yourself. If you're still up when we get home, we could make some popcorn . . . " Impulsively, she gave LD a hug. "I'm glad you're here, LD. I gotta go, though. Bye . . . "

After Lucy was gone, LD walked from room to room, looking at everything. She looked in the fridge, but didn't eat anything.

Then she went upstairs and looked in the closet. Lucy had cleared out half of it, but her bright wardrobe threatened to spill out into the empty space. LD did not unpack anything. After a while, although she wasn't sleepy, she went to bed and read *Building for the Stage*.

When Lucy and her father came home late, LD was asleep. Lucy tiptoed in and got ready for bed in the darkness. All the while she did so, she listened to the sound of LD breathing. It made her quietly happy.

CHAPTER 15

Yick was sitting in the cafeteria staring into space when Heather stopped by his table. "Hi, Yick," she said. "Are you working backstage tonight?"

"Tonight? What's tonight?"

"LD says we need an extra work party. She says we're falling behind our schedule and we've got to try to catch up. Didn't you know about it?"

"Uh, yeah, I guess I did. But I'm not coming. Rick's brother knows a guy who's got a siren we can use, and we're going to get it and try it out."

Heather made a face. "I wish I had your excuse. I thought working on the crew was going to be a good time, but LD has gotten really weird lately."

Yick shrugged. "She's sort of under pressure, I guess."

"Under pressure! She's like the gorilla on her hard hat! Anyway, I won't have to be around backstage so much anymore. I'm helping to make posters and programs. It's a big improvement! You ought to do that, too . . . "

She went and sat down, leaving Yick thinking about his job of arranging the effects. It was true that LD had become a difficult taskmaster, but he was having a great time fooling around with the lights and noises and starter's pistol (which had an interesting quality when it was fired next to a bass drum from the school band). The only time he had any real conflict with LD was when she pressed him about the ghost . . .

"Okay," Ms. Avery called, "Eddy, after that speech, you leave — exit, stage right."

Wheels peered into the darkness beyond the stage. Ms. Avery was only a shadowy form in a chair on the gym floor, which someday would be in the third row of the audience. "Right away?" he asked.

"Of course! You're following Carmen. So get out of there."

Wheels turned and went into the wings, where he found Lucy standing by the prop

114

table. "Hi," he said. "I'm supposed to be following you."

"Great," she said. "Want some?" She offered him a glass of cola she had brought in from the cafeteria when the rehearsal was starting.

Before he could answer, Stephanie appeared from the shadows. "Hi, Wheels," she said, bestowing on him her most brilliant smile.

"Oh, hi, Steph," Lucy said. "I didn't know you were there."

"You bet," Steph said. "Just waiting for my cue, you know. Hey, Wheels, nice shirt!" He was wearing a sleeveless Cannibals' t-shirt, part of his costume, for the first time today.

"You like it?"

"Oh, sure," Steph said enthusiastically. "it makes you look so . . . *tough*." She widened her eyes a little when she said the word.

"I think that's your cue, Steph," Lucy interrupted.

"Is it? Oh, yeah. Thanks. See you later, Wheels . . . "

Lucy watched her go. "Are you sure you don't want a sip?" she asked Wheels again.

"Aw, no — thanks, that's okay . . . "

"Go ahead," she said. "Aren't you thirsty?"

"Well, yeah, I am," Wheels said, accepting the glass.

"It's probably warm by now."

"That's okay." Wheels tipped a slug of lukewarm pop into his mouth. Then, in a sudden explosion, he sprayed it on the stage floor. "Gahh! What's that?"

"What's wrong?"

"There's something in it!" He peered at the floor in the half-light. "Something alive. I could feel it wiggling. It's a worm or — oh, gross, it's somebody's shoelace!"

"A shoelace!? How did that get in there?"

"I don't believe it," Wheels said. He picked the sodden lace off the floor and disgustedly draped it across one corner of the table. "We'll be lucky if we don't get athlete's mouth. You could probably sue someone for a million bucks!"

Just then Joey came off stage. As he walked, his right shoe flopped laceless. "Hi, guys," he said. "How's it going?"

"Oh, very funny, Joey," Wheels said. "Your sense of humor kills me. Almost."

Joey looked blank. "What are you talking about?"

Wheels held up the dripping shoelace.

"Hey," Joey said. "Wheels, my man, you found my shoelace. Where was it?"

"Oh, right," Wheels said. "You wouldn't know, would you? You've got no idea how it got into Lucy's Coke."

"What? I never put it there! Give me that!" He snatched the shoelace out of

116

Wheels' hand. "Some jerk took my lace, that's all. I don't know how it got in her drink."

"Sure," Wheels said. "Sure. That makes perfect sense, doesn't it, Lucy? I mean, if you — "

"Wheels! Pay attention!" Susie was yelling at him from the other side of the stage. "That's your cue! Get out there!"

Wheels looked at Lucy. "See you later," he said, and strode onstage past Joey.

"Look," Joey said to Lucy, "I didn't have anything to do with it, and that's the truth. Do you want me to get you another Coke?"

She glanced at him nervously and then fixed her eyes firmly on the action onstage. "No, thanks," she said. "It's fine. Anyway, the cafeteria's closed."

Joey hovered beside her for a moment, but Lucy wouldn't look at him. Finally he wandered away, his face frozen in an expressionless mask, his eyes glittering darkly.

"Make yourselves comfortable," Ms. Avery said. "I've got a few notes to give you before you go."

The cast flopped down on the stage and waited. Half a dozen found room on the old mattress that someone had dragged in as a prop. Joey sat apart on an old plastic milk crate, hugging one knee to his chest.

"On the whole," Ms. Avery said, "things are going well. With the usual amount of superhuman effort and some luck, we might actually be ready for opening night. Most of you are doing pretty well with your lines. But Joey and Steph, you both need to do a lot more work on yours. We should be off the book and moving around already, so you'd better buckle down.

"Also, I can tell that most of you are putting some thought into your characters, and I appreciate that. Lucy, you're making Carmen dreamy and romantic right now, which is certainly part of her nature. But remember that she is also desperate and driven. Do you know what I mean?"

Lucy thought for a second. "It's like she's only got once chance."

"Yes," Ms. Avery said. "That's it. In fact, it's like she had *no* chance until Eddy came along. So she wants to grab this opportunity with both hands. But if she grabs too hard, she knows she'll crush it and have nothing."

"Okay." Lucy nodded.

"Wheels," Ms. Avery said, "most of the time, you've got just enough swagger and self-assurance. But when you get around Carmen, you turn into a pussycat!"

Everyone laughed.

"She won't bite. I don't think she will, anyway. And if she does, you've got to bite back. In other words, you've got to be bolder.

All right? Joey, your version of Lucky is good. Just work on those lines. Stephanie, your character hasn't started to form at all yet. How come?"

Steph floundered for an answer. Before she could find one, Ms. Avery continued. "The key to Mrs. Wark is that she knows exactly how Carmen feels. She was once Carmen's age, and felt as Carmen feels. But she got trapped. She wants her daughter to be something she never was, but she isn't sure how that can be. Her dilemma is that she doesn't know if she should encourage Carmen's feelings for Eddy or not. If you can keep that in mind and learn your lines by next week, you'll make me the happiest director in Degrassi Junior High. Okay?"

"Sure. No problem."

"Great. Then that's it for today. I'll see you all next week."

Everyone got up and began to head for the green room where a pile of coats, boots and books waited.

"Oh, and Stephanie," Ms. Avery said, "one more thing. I know you haven't really started to move around yet, because you've been tied to the book. But when you do, remember that women like Mrs. Wark are *tired*. Think of the most tired you've ever been and multiply it by two. It's hard to pick up your feet, it's hard to walk across the room. Everything is an effort. Okay?"

"Sure," Stephanie said again. "Thanks." That part should be a cinch. She was already tired of the whole play.

"And don't worry about your part," Ms. Avery concluded. "You'll be fine once you've got your lines memorized."

When she got to the green room, Stephanie spotted Wheels with his coat already on, hanging around by the outside door. Inside the green room, Lucy was getting ready to leave. "Hi, Mom!" Lucy said when she saw her.

"Oh," Steph said, "great acting, Luce. Right in character. That's going to win rave reviews for sure."

Lucy gave her a quizzical look. "What's wrong with you?"

"I suppose you're going to take off and do a little method acting with Wheels now, are you?"

Lucy glanced quickly at the open doorway. "Look, Steph, we're just going for a Coke, okay? It's no big deal."

"Oh, sure. Just a Coke. And then maybe back to your place to work on lines and of course you didn't know there wouldn't be anyone home, but there never is, is there? For your information, Lucy, Wheels and I got very close last term. And if you're going to use this stupid play as an excuse to move in on him, then — " Stephanie's eyes filled suddenly with hot tears. Grabbing her coat and bag, she bolted from the room.

Lucy followed more slowly. When she got to Wheels, still standing aimlessly by the door, she said, "Listen, Wheels — I just remembered I'm supposed to see my social worker this afternoon. So I can't go for very long, okay?"

"You mean we can't work on lines later?"

"Not today. Maybe some other time . . . "

Because it was Arthur's night to come to his mother's, Stephanie allowed him to walk home with her. During first term, she would have driven him off with violence, but lately she had discovered, through painful experience, that a friend — and a brother — were sometimes very comforting. In any case, after her outburst in front of Lucy, she felt too drained to do violence to a dishcloth, let alone Arthur.

After they had walked in silence for a while, Arthur said, "It's me, isn't it?"

"What are you talking about?"

"It's because I play your son that you can't get into the play."

A wave of affection for him startled her. "No. That isn't it. It's got nothing to do with you."

"I just thought that it might be difficult to call me my son, and stuff like that."

She looked at him reflectively for a moment. "Is it hard for you to call me mother?"

121

"Oh, no," he said. "It's easy. You always tell me what to do anyway."

She surprised herself by laughing. "I guess that's why I don't really have any trouble talking to you like a son. I thought it would be awful, but it isn't . . . "

"Then what's the problem?"

She gave him a withering look, "Oh, right," he said. "It's Wheels and Lucy."

"It should be me," she said. "I should have had that part. It isn't fair."

"But what can you do about it?"

She paused. "I can declare war about it, that's what. I'm not going to give up without a fight."

Arthur looked at her uneasily. "Uh, what are you going to do?"

"Everything in the book," she replied. "Everything I can think of."

At that moment Wheels, Lucy, Heather and Erica were sitting in a booth at the malt shop.

"Have you noticed," Erica said, "how this play is changing people?"

"What do you mean?" asked Wheels.

Before Erica could reply, Heather spoke up. "Well, look at Erica, for example," she said. "Wouldn't you say she's changed?"

Wheels stared at Erica. He knew, for some girl-reason he did not understand, that he was supposed to see some change in her, but she seemed exactly the same as always to him. "No," he admitted at last. "I don't see any difference."

Heather grinned maliciously at her sister, who responded by throwing paper napkins at her. "Shut up, Heather. Just shut up."

"Is Erica different?" Wheels persisted.

Erica looked at Heather and said, "I'll kill you." Then she said to Wheels, "Forget it. She doesn't know what she's talking about."

"Okay. But I've sure seen a change in Joey," Wheels said, and he told the story of the shoelace in Lucy's drink.

"Ooh, gross!" Heather said.

"Completely gross," Wheels affirmed. "I mean, Joey was always sort of off the wall with his jokes and stuff, but this is too much. I felt like I had inhaled a giant tape worm or something. It's bad enough it was a sweaty old shoelace."

"But are you sure he did it?" asked Heather. "He could be telling the truth.

"Who else could it have been?" Wheels demanded.

"I don't know. Anyone. Strange things go on backstage, you know. Anyway, *why* would Joey want to do it?"

"Well, he might have wanted to play a trick on me," Lucy said.

"What for?"

She told them about Joey's call the other

night. "Maybe it hurt his feelings when I didn't make time for him. It's the only thing I can think of."

Just then Joey walked in. Seeing them, he walked over to their table. "Hi, guys," he said. "What's happening?"

Heather was the only one to respond. "Hi, Joey."

"Hey, what gives?" Joey looked around the table, but no one had anything to say. "I get it," he said. "Polar bear country. Real nice friends. What's with you guys?"

"Real friends don't put shoelaces in other people's drinks," Wheels said.

"I never did it, man! I told you that!"

"Sure," Wheels said. "Sure."

"Ahh, you're crazy," Joey said. "What's the use of talking to you!" And he turned and walked out.

"See what I mean?" Erica said. "He's just like Lucky."

"No, he isn't," Heather said. "I believe him." But no one else at the table did.

After dinner, Arthur said, "Can I watch television? There's a hockey game on. Poor people like to watch hockey."

His mother leaned back in her chair and fingered the handle of her teacup. "Is that in the play?" she asked. "What about poor people doing the dishes?"

"Poor people don't have dishes," Arthur

said. "They scoop food out of cans with their hands."

"It's okay, Mom," Stephanie said. "I'll do them."

"Great!" Arthur disappeared through the door to the living room. "Thanks, Steph!"

Stephanie got up and began to stack the dishes while her mother continued to drink her tea. After a moment, her mother said, "How's the play going?"

Steph made a face.

"Not so good? How come?"

"I don't think I like acting . . . "

"Mm, you liked the idea well enough before rehearsals started. Maybe you don't like the part you've got."

"Well . . . maybe," Steph said, and then burst out, "I don't *feel* like a mother! How am I supposed to be a mother to kids my own age?"

"Oh, I think you could be a very good mother, Stephanie."

"But I don't want to!"

Mrs. Kaye studied her daughter for a moment. "Do you think mothers always want to?"

"Huh?"

"You heard me. Do you think mothers always want to look after their kids? Get them dressed in the morning? Feed them? Make sure their homework is done?" She looked at the plate in Stephanie's hand. "Wash the dishes?"

"I don't know . . . . No. I suppose not."

Mrs. Kaye poured herself another cup of tea. "Sweetheart, I'm not trying to lay anything on you, but lots of times, being a parent means doing what you don't want to do, just because that's the way it has to be." She smiled. "Sometimes, on good days, you remember you're doing it because you love your kids. But most of the time, you don't even think about it. You just do what you have to do." She stood up. "Here," she said. "I'll give you a hand with those. Do you want to wash or dry?"

CHAPTER 16

"Students are reminded," the intercom said, "That our play, *Blood and Moonlight,* will be playing for four nights only. Rumors that the production will be moved to Broadway are a complete fabrication . . . "

When Arthur saw Yick that morning, he was trying unsuccessfully to push his way through a wall. He was doing this because he was carrying a brown paper parcel so large he couldn't see over it. Instead of pushing against a door, he was wedged against the wall beside it.

"Yick," said Arthur, "over here." He guided Yick through the door into the hallway.

"Thanks, Arthur," Yick said. "it's sort of hard to navigate, carrying all this stuff."

"What is it?" Arthur asked.

"A ghost," Yick said, and added firmly, "a play ghost."

When they reached Yick's locker, he dropped the parcel and started rummaging in his pockets. Finally, after rejecting pens, coins, string, a loop of wire, three rubber bands, an old bus transfer and a comb, he dug out a crumpled slip of paper. Consulting this, he began to open his lock.

"I still haven't memorized my new combination," he explained.

In a second, the lock snicked open. Yick swung the door wide. Then his jaw fell open as well. Sitting on the unusual mound of junk at the bottom was a large plastic pineapple.

"Arthur," Yick said, "tell me you did this." The pineapple had google eyes and a big red mouth, and was wearing a hat covered with other kinds of plastic fruit.

"I didn't do it, Yick. I don't know how to get into your locker."

"Then where did this come from?" Yick stared tensely at the pineapple. He looked like he was ready to drop a match in his locker and send the whole thing up in flames.

"Have you considered the possibility of a time-warp?"

Reluctantly, Yick got close enough to hang up his jacket. Then he picked up the pineapple as if it were a disease and closed the locker. "It's more like a mind-warp," he said.

"Weird city. Anyway, I've got to take this stuff backstage. I'll see you later."

The shop was a scene of slightly modified chaos. Annie was struggling with giant bolts of canvas and a staple gun. Along one wall, the canvas-covered flats were slowly accumulating, while on the floor, the skeleton of the turntable was nearly finished. The small crew gathered round, however, when Yick began to unwrap his version of the ghost.

Inside the brown paper, there were several smaller packages. Yick opened the largest, and brought out a clear plastic raincoat and a black one.

"This is going to be the ghost itself," he said. "We hang the clear raincoat on top of the black one. That way, we only see the stab wound when the ghost is pulled around backwards." Then he held up a package of white balloons. "These can be the head. We can draw a face on one of these with make-up . . . and put *this* on top." He unearthed a glowing orange and green fright wig. Then he produced a couple of pulleys, and a large roll of light nylon fishing line. "And this is how we can move it on and off stage, and turn it around to show the wound." He glanced nervously around the assembled group. "What do you think?"

Annie said, "Is Wheels going to be scared of a raincoat? And what's this pineapple for?" She held up the plastic pineapple Yick had found in his locker.

"The pineapple has nothing to do with it," Yick said. "It's just a joke."

Annie looked at him strangely. "You've got a weird sense of humor," she said, putting the pineapple back on the table.

"I think the ghost could work," Shane said. "If it's sort of dark, you know . . . "

"Dark!" Snake said with sudden inspiration. "We can run it in black light! Then it won't look like a raincoat at all. And the wig will show up like a searchlight! I bet we can find make-up for black light, too. Glowing blood for the stab wound in the back!"

LD had been looking at the unpacking without speaking. She still had concerns about the turntable. Now she said, "Yeah, I like the black light. Is the ghost going to be silent?"

Yick was caught off guard. He hadn't thought about ghostly noises — just ghostly looks. "I don't know," he said. "What does a ghost sound like?"

"Oh," Annie said, "it groans and shrieks!"

Yick looked unhappy. "I'm . . . um . . . not very good at groaning and shrieking."

"I suppose we could record something," Snake said. "But it's better if it's live."

"Come on, Yick," Annie said with relish. "Just imagine the ghost is putting its icy cold fingers around your neck! Wouldn't you just scream?"

Yick edged away from her. "I can't scream very loud," he lied. "Something genetic. All my family is like that."

LD looked at Snake. "Couldn't you play something?"

Snake laughed. "Hey, our music isn't that bad, LD," he said. "But maybe you're right. I could get groans out of Wheels' bass, and shrieks out of my guitar."

LD thought for a moment. "And you think you can get an ultraviolet light rigged up?"

"Sure," Snake said. "Nothing to it."

"Okay," she concluded. "Then we've got a ghost. Thanks, Yick. Once we get the sets up, you can string it up and try it out. No, on second thought, that might be too late. You can do a trial run once Snake has the black light hung." She was about to turn away when she spotted a small unopened package beneath the raincoat. "What's that?"

"Nothing," Yick said quickly, and shoved the bag in his pocket. "It's my lunch."

"It's four o'clock in the afternoon," LD said. "Didn't you eat?"

"Too excited," Yick said. "Too busy. Ghosts, you know." He laughed nervously. "Okay, I've got to go now." And he quickly folded up the ghostly paraphernalia. As he made good his escape from the shop, he

131

touched his pocket to make sure the package was still there. It didn't contain his lunch, of course, but something much more important. But he couldn't tell anyone what it was. They just wouldn't understand ...

It was after six when LD changed her hard hat for her regular cap, closed the shop and walked out into the late winter gloom. The flats — the canvas-covered walls on which the scenes would be painted — were coming along slowly and steadily, but she wasn't so sure about the turntable. She had used as much wood as she could spare to make it as stiff as possible, but it was beginning to look as though Snake's criticism was right. If she didn't come up with a solution, the whole thing might have to be lifted and turned by hand.

For a moment she had an image of about twenty students scurrying onstage every time a scene came to an end. It would sort of change the play. Maybe if the set movers dressed up as Munchkins, they could make the play over into the Wizard of Oz ...

The thought didn't cheer her up, though. Instead, she was submerged by a wave of longing for her father. Not that he could do anything about the sets. But at least she would have someone to give her a hug and tell her things were all right.

CHAPTER 17

The bell rang, and the grade eight class came to sudden life, slamming books shut, erupting in talk, and flowing, like a thawed stream, toward the door. "LD," Mr. Raditch called. "Could you come here for a moment, please?"

Reluctantly she walked to the front of the room and stood before his desk. She was relieved, though, to see him closing his brief-case and carefully wiping chalk dust from his fingers. She knew he would not keep her long.

"I just wanted to tell you, LD," he said, "that your work is getting marginal again. If we weren't so close to opening day for the play, I would have to think seriously about taking you out of the production."

"Well, I've been sort of busy trying to get everything built," she said defensively. "It hasn't exactly been easy."

"I understand that," he replied. "But we had an agreement that you would keep your marks up. If they fall much further, even the credit from this work won't save your year." He picked up his briefcase and prepared to leave. "And, don't forget. Your job isn't necessarily to build everything yourself. It's to *get* it built."

A few minutes later LD stood in front of her locker, staring at a list taped to the inside of the door. It was her personal bulletin board, and it carried such cryptic legends as: "Hubnuts — $^3/_8$ × 12' . . . 3pts. white/ 1 pt. green . . . front steps . . . Check spook! . . . flats/props/costumes/blood . . . sirens? . . ." Beside it was a handmade calendar that went until opening day. One by one the days had been crossed off. There was now a little over a week to go. After a long study of the list, and then of the calendar, she declared, "It's hopeless."

"What?"

She turned to Lucy, who was just closing her locker. "I said it's hopeless. I don't see how we can get everything ready."

"Really?"

"I've been telling everyone we have to work harder, but it seems the harder I push,

134

the slower they go. In fact, there's hardly any 'they' to push anymore. Mostly it's just me and Snake, and he's busy with the lights. And now Mr. Raditch is on my case about my school work. I don't know what to do."

"Well," Lucy said, "why didn't you tell Mr. Raditch? He could make them help you. They're supposed to work if they want credit."

"They are working," LD said gloomily. "On everything else. Maybe if I just stay in the shop from now until the opening . . . "

"You mean, sleep there?"

"Yeah. I might get it all done . . . "

"Oh, come on," Lucy said. "That's a really dumb idea. Why don't you just learn everyone's lines, and put the play on yourself?"

"Thanks, Lucy," LD said drily, "that makes me feel a lot better . . . "

"Well," Lucy said, "you're not the only one involved. If it flops, then everyone has egg on their face. Anyway, you have to take some time off tomorrow night."

The hallway was emptying quickly, but LD noticed Wheels appear at the far end, heading toward them. "Tomorrow night? What's tomorrow night?" she asked.

"It's my birthday," Lucy said. "My mom and dad are taking me out for dinner after rehearsal, and you have to come."

"I can't," LD said. "Too much to do. Why not take him?" And she pointed to Wheels, who had just come up behind Lucy.

"Take me where?" said Wheels.

"Out for dinner on her birthday," LD said. "Tomorrow."

"Tomorrow's your birthday?" Wheels said. "Hey, I didn't know that. That — "

"Wheels!" He was interrupted by Stephanie calling from the other end of the hall. "Susie's looking for you!" He hesitated, and she said, "Right now! It's important. Something about your costume."

"Uh . . . okay," he said. "I'll see you guys later."

When he had disappeared down the stairwell with Stephanie, LD closed her locker. "Great timing, eh?"

"Oh, yeah," Lucy said. "And I bet Susie will be real surprised to see him, too."

"You mean, she isn't really looking for him?"

"What do you think? That girl has got some kind of radar. Every time I get within half a mile of Wheels now, she shows up to spoil the party. Come on — let's go be theatrical. At least she doesn't interrupt when Wheels and I are on stage together."

When she got to the shop, the speech LD had been preparing, about working long and hard, pitching in and pulling together, and making the deadline of opening night, suddenly seemed to her like a waste of time. There was a scribbled note from Annie wait-

136

ing for her, that said she was out putting up posters and would not be back. Spike and Heather were nowhere to be seen. Shane had not returned since starting to paint a flat the week before. Only Snake and Yick were around. Yick was patiently trying to unknot a piece of fishing line, while Snake hauled spotlights from a storage cupboard to the stage.

Dejectedly, LD set to work to hammer home the plywood skin of her turntable — an object she had come to hate. It seemed obvious to her that even with the stiff plywood in place, it was going to flop all around the edges, and the smooth bearings of the hub would be absolutely useless. She was about half done when Snake sauntered by, carrying a couple of lights and a sheaf of colored gels. He paused, but LD refused to look up. After a moment he went on, and she savagely hammered another nail into place.

When Snake brought the spotlights onstage, he was just in time to see calamity in progress. As always there was a rehearsal going on, but Snake had been quietly working around the actors, hanging lights and focusing them with the aid of a tall stepladder. Also working in the shadows, Yick was coping with swarms of fine nylon line, hooking up his pulleys and preparing the track of his ghost. But as Snake appeared, he saw Yick reeling the line tight and unwittingly tipping the stepladder over with a stray loop of the line.

Snake yelled, "Hey! Look out!" as the ladder swayed, tilted and then fell with a swish and a gunshot bang on the stage, narrowly missing Wheels.

"Wow!" Wheels leaped like a startled mountain goat, and whirled to see where the ladder had come from. The first person he saw was Joey, standing open-mouthed in the wings. Astonishment mingled with rage on Wheel's face. "You stupid jerk — !" Blind with anger, he started for Joey like a struck batter charging the pitcher's mound.

"Whoa, wait a minute!" Still lugging lights, Snake lumbered forward and managed to put himself between the two just in time. "Take it easy, Wheels. Joey didn't have anything to do with it."

By now a crowd had gathered, and Joey had found his voice. "Are you out of your mind?" he said. "What makes you think *I* did it?"

Wheel's face was dark with anger. "Well," he said aggressively. "Didn't you?"

"No," said Snake. "That's what I'm telling you. It was an accident. Yick's fishing line pulled the ladder over."

Wheels seemed to see Snake for the first time. "Is that right?" He looked at Yick who stood nearby, holding a cloud of transparent line.

Yick said, "I'm sorry. I didn't see it."

Slowly Wheels deflated. Finally, he looked at Joey. "Sorry," he said shortly. "I was just shook up, I guess."

"Yeah, sure," Joey said. "No problem." But he did not look directly at Wheels when he said it.

When the rehearsal ended later that afternoon, Lucy went into the shop to see if LD was ready to go home. She found her glumly driving in the last nail of the turntable. Snake appeared and stood beside them, watching. After one final, tired blow, LD stood up. All three looked at the broad circle in silence. A moment passed, and Snake cautiously stretched out one toe to nudge the rim. Nothing happened. He pushed harder. Still the wheel did not move. Then he bent, gripped the edge with both hands and shoved. The wheel groaned to life, slid a few inches and then grated to a shuddering halt.

"Well," he said, "it does turn . . . "

"Oh, shut up!" LD exploded. "It's a wreck! A mess! It was a stupid idea from the beginning, and there's nothing we can do about it." She tossed her hammer onto the platform with a clatter and tore off her apron and hard hat. "I quit!"

"But LD," Snake said, "you can't — "

"Yes, I can!" She thrust the hard hat into his hands. "Here! You're in charge." And before he could reply, she dashed out of the shop. Lucy shook her head and followed her.

For a long moment Snake stared at the door. Then he slowly bent to the turntable and pulled at it thoughtfully, listening to the bottom grind across the concrete floor.

The next day, on her way back from lunch, Lucy ran into Wheels a block from school. She was surprised to see him there, because his house was in the other direction.

"Hi," he said, starting to walk along with her. "Happy birthday."

"Thank you," she said. "Nice of you to remember."

He laughed a little nervously. "Well, I only found out yesterday. It would be hard to forget in one day, wouldn't it?"

Lucy looked at him. "That depends, doesn't it?"

A little color came into his face. "Well, anyway, I got you a present." He handed her a small box. "I didn't have time to wrap it, but I thought I'd give it to you when I could, since we seem to get interrupted so often . . . "

"A present? That's really sweet! Thank you!" She took the box from him and held it in her hand. It was about three inches square, with a gold foil lid. When she slipped this off, she found inside a silver pin sitting on black velvet. The pin was round, about the size of a dime, and had a serene, stylized face engraved on it. "It's beautiful!" she said. "Thank you!"

"I think it looks like the moon," he said. "So it seemed right for you. You know, because of the play."

"You're right," she said. "It is the moon. I want to wear it — " She peered inside her coat collar, but she was wearing a fuzzy, open-knit sweater. "Oh, it won't really work on this. But I'll wear it later. I'll wear it inside my costume when we put the play on — for luck." She gave him a wide smile, and thought about giving him a kiss, too. She held back, though. They were in front of the school by now, and she was afraid of drawing enemy fire from the ramparts above. Besides, public kisses were never as real as private ones . . .

Stephanie heard about the pin from Heather and Erica. Lucy had shown it to them in the girls' washroom.

"Get serious," Stephanie said. "He wouldn't give her jewelry. They're not going out." But she knew, with leaden certainty, that they were telling the truth.

"We saw it," Heather said. "A little silver moon."

"Are you sure she didn't buy it herself, and say she got it from Wheels?"

"Oh, come on, Steph," Erica said. "Why don't you just accept it? Wheels likes Lucy. Not you. Not me. You can't change that."

Stephanie bit her lip. "It's just a phase. He's stage struck, but he'll get over it." And she walked proudly away, her head high, her heart in fragments on the floor behind her.

Later, when Steph went backstage, Wheels and Lucy were already in their warm-up, working side by side on the stage. Miserably she went into the green room to drop her coat, and saw Lucy's coat lying on the couch. From one pocket protruded the gold corner of a box. Stephanie glanced quickly over her shoulder, and then, unable to stop herself, pulled out the box and opened it. The silver pin lay nestled in the velvet, just as the twins had described it.

For a moment she stared at it, and then, suddenly, she threw the box against the wall with all her strength, and stormed from the room. *Who cares?* she raged to herself. *Who cares? If he thinks she's so great, who wants him? Stupid boy, stupid play, stupid Lucy, stupid, stupid, stupid!*

"Ms. Avery," Lucy said, "I can't find my pin!"

Ms. Avery and Susie both looked up from the paperwork they had spread across the front of the stage.

"Where did you leave it?" the teacher asked.

"It was in my coat pocket. I'm sure of it. I put it there when I started my warm-up."

"And where was your coat?"

"In the green room."

Ms. Avery looked concerned. "I'll mention it when we start again," she said, "and maybe someone will find it. I can't believe anyone in the cast would take it." She looked at her watch. "We'd better get going. Susie, can you get Melanie, Arthur and Voula onstage for me? We'll start from their scene, and go on through to the end of the act. And ask everyone if they've seen Lucy's pin, too."

But no one knew where it was. Later, Lucy and Wheels were sitting cross-legged on a table in the wings, waiting to go on. Stephanie, miserable around them, but unable to be anywhere else, sat on a milk crate nearby. "I'm really upset about that pin," Lucy said. "Even the box is gone."

Wheels had been systematically reducing a Styrofoam cup to granular snow. Now he said grimly, "I bet we could find it if we searched everyone."

"You think someone took it?"

"Don't you? Who's been causing all the trouble back here since the play started?"

"Who?" said Steph.

"Who else?" Wheels said. "Mr. Lucky. Lucky the slime. The weasel of Degrassi Junior High."

"I thought Joey was your friend!" Stephanie was horrified to hear Wheels attacking Joey, especially since she knew he was innocent.

"He was. But he's been acting weird since the play began. Haven't you seen it? He sneaks around playing tricks on people. Frankly, I don't trust him anymore."

"But — Joey wouldn't steal Lucy's pin! Why should he?"

"I wouldn't put it past him. I don't care what Snake says, I still think he had something to do with that ladder, and *that* nearly killed me. So, a little pin, when no one's looking — "

"Lucy! Wheels!" Susie called. "You're on now."

They went onstage, leaving Stephanie feeling sick. She had never been close to Joey, but he was a friend. Now Wheels was slamming him unfairly. For months Wheels had been everything bright and desirable to her. Now his suspicions made her feel sticky and unclean.

Unhappily, she climbed off the crate and walked toward the green room.

When she got there, she was startled to find it torn apart and deserted. Coats and books were stacked in the middle of the floor, all the cushions were thrown off the couch and chairs, and the couch was pushed out from the wall. Then she saw a hand on the back of the couch, and she realized there was someone lying down behind it. Before she could move, there was a minor upheaval, and the hand pulled a very dusty Joey into view. In his other hand he held a small box, and a silver pin with a bit of gray fluff hanging from it.

"Stephanie!" He was surprised to see her.

"Uh . . . hi, Joey. What . . . ?"

"Oh, I found Lucy's pin. I thought it might have fallen out of her pocket, so I looked under all the cushions. Then I looked behind the couch. The box was there, but the pin wasn't. I found it down a heat vent. She's lucky. It could have disappeared forever."

"But — Joey, that's really sweet! You've got to give it to her. She'll be so happy!" She hadn't thought anything when she threw the box away. It had just been a fit of anger. But then she hadn't been able to tell anyone. Now Joey, who was being blamed for taking the pin, had saved it from oblivion. "Take it to her right now," she said.

He was still holding the pin in the palm of his hand. At her suggestion, a shadow crossed his face. He hesitated. "Uh, no. You better give it to her."

"But why?!"

He tipped the pin into her hand and handed her the box. "I know what they think," he said, looking sad and old. "Wheels and Lucy and some others. If I show up with it, they'll think I took it. You take it to her, okay? Don't tell her I found it. I'm going to put the cushions back . . . "

He turned to start tidying up. Steph bit her lip, and then slowly walked back to the stage. It was even more difficult for *her* to give the pin back — but she really had no choice.

" — must have fallen behind the couch," Steph said vaguely when she gave the pin back to Lucy. "Too bad about the dust. It's a really nice pin. And, Lucy — I've been meaning to talk to you. About you and Wheels. Don't you think it would be good for the play if you got a little closer? I mean, as Eddy, he needs to loosen up a bit, right? Of course, I used to be crazy about him, but I've sort of changed, so don't let that stand in your way. Why don't you spend some time with him . . . ?"

When LD came home that night, after a long solitary, brooding walk, she found Lucy and Wheels sitting on the sofa in the living room. They were both holding scripts — and there *was* enough light to read by — but if she had thought about it, she would have realized they had memorized their lines and abandoned their scripts three weeks ago. But

LD didn't think about it. She had made herself go numb, after her defeat in the shop. So while Wheels and Lucy sat in the living room hoping she would go away, she grabbed a bag of cheese corn and a diet cherry cola and stumbled upstairs to bed.

CHAPTER 18

LD struggled upward through heavy layers of sleep, like trying to clamber out of a pile of warm sand. Before she reached the surface, the knocking came again and she heard the voice of Lucy's mother calling through the door.

"LD! Your father's on the phone!"

The words didn't wake her mind up, but they sent a jolt of electricity through her body. She shot out of bed, grabbed her dressing gown and tumbled into the hall in the space of time it took to open her eyes. Lucy's mother, holding her own robe tight around her, said, "You can take it downstairs, honey. I'll hang up when you get on the line."

Numbly, LD jolted down the stairs, struggling into her robe. As she went, thoughts began to flow through her mind. What had happened? Was her father all right?

In the kitchen, she picked up the white handset. "Hello?"

There was a click as Lucy's mother hung up the bedroom extension. Then a voice said, "LD?"

LD tried to make the voice sound like her father, but failed. "Yeah?" she said.

"It's me," the voice said. "Snake."

"Snake?" she said stupidly. What had happened to her father? And what was Snake doing in Corsica?

"I told Lucy's mom I was your dad," Snake said. "I didn't think she'd let me talk to you, otherwise."

LD finally began to wake up. She stared at the clock on the stove. 2:36. "Are you crazy?" she said. "What are you calling at 2:30 in the morning for?"

"Take it easy," Snake said. "I got an idea and I had to call you. Are you ready for this?"

LD was starting to get mad. "Listen, Snake . . . "

"No, you listen, LD. This is it. Casters."

There was a short silence. "What?"

"Casters," Snake repeated. "That's the answer."

LD looked at the telephone. Great, she thought. It's the middle of the night and I'm listening to a crazy person. "What are you talking about?"

"The turntable, of course. All it needs is some casters and it will work fine. You know — those wheel things they put on beds and pianos?"

There was another short silence while LD digested this idea. "Yeah," she said finally. "Sure. I get it. Casters. Can I go back to bed now?"

"Hey, no problem," Snake said. "See you tomorrow."

"Yeah," LD said, and added grudgingly, "thanks."

When she went back upstairs, Lucy's mother came out of her bedroom. "Is everything all right?" she asked.

LD had forgotten that she was supposed to be talking to her father. "Uh . . . yeah," she said vaguely, "fine. He just . . . wanted to say hello."

"That's good," said Mrs. Baines. "The climate must be agreeing with him in Corsica. He sounded quite a bit younger than when he left . . . "

When LD got back into bed, Lucy sat up. "What's going on? Was that your dad?"

"No," LD said shortly. "It was Snake."

"Snake? In the middle of the night? What did he want?"

"He had some stupid idea about the platform. I don't know. It might work." LD balled herself up under the covers.

Lucy paused. "LD, sometimes you act

really dumb, you know that?"

There was another pause, and then LD began to reappear. "What?"

"I just don't see why you're so hard on Snake. He really likes you, you know. In fact, I think he's crazy about you."

LD's head lifted from the pillow. "*Snake?*"

"Of course, Snake! Didn't you know that?"

"How can you tell?" LD was wide awake again. She struggled upright and stared at Lucy.

"Well, for one thing, he's the only member of the crew left. Everybody else has taken off because you've been so hard on them."

"But . . . " LD let her head sink back against the head of the bed. Lucy's words brought on a flood of images, of times when she had chewed out one member of the crew or another. It had been necessary, hadn't it? She'd been in charge. How else could she get everything done?

"And if you weren't so busy being the boss, you might notice the way he looks at you. Even if you don't want to go out with him," Lucy said, "you could at least be friends. If what you say about the sets and stuff is true, you could use a friend right now. I mean, he's even lying awake nights thinking about you, for heaven's sake! What more do you want?"

In a little while, Lucy was asleep again,

and LD lay awake. She didn't want to sleep yet. She had some things to think about.

LD looked around the table and took a deep breath. Getting the crew together hadn't been easy. Almost everyone had offered an excuse of some sort, and she had had to push to get them all to come. It made her realize that what she was about to say was long overdue.

"Okay," she said, "this won't take long. I called this meeting because I might as well say this just once. We've got less than a week to go until opening night, and we're nowhere near ready."

The others shifted uneasily. Annie doodled determinedly on the back of her binder. Yick stared hard at the scarred table top. Finally Shane said, "So?"

"So, the reason we aren't ready," LD said, "is me."

Annie's pen stopped moving. Yick forgot about the table top. Everyone was suddenly looking at LD.

"Mr. Raditch put me in charge, and I've been just horrible to everyone ever since. I'm sorry. I thought it was the way to get things done, but I was wrong. So, I want someone else to take over. I'll still work back here and everything, so we can get the show up on time, but somebody else should be the boss. Not me."

She stopped and looked around the table again. Nobody said anything. Finally, she said, "Snake? What about you?"

Snake shook his head. "I don't think so, LD. I think you're in charge. But thanks for the apology." He looked at the others. "We just need to know what to do. If everyone else is willing to work, that is."

There was a pause, and then Heather said, "Sure. I don't mind working. I just don't like getting chewed out."

"Me, too," Spike said. Now it was LD who was caught off guard. She had expected someone else to give the orders after her speech. "Ah . . . well, we need to put casters on the turntable," she grinned at Snake, "so it will work the way it's supposed to. And try out the ghost. Finish painting the flats and mount them on the platform . . . "

In a moment, everyone was up and working — all but Snake, who took an extra minute to walk over to LD and put the hard hat back on her head. "Here you go, chief," he said. "Gorilla my dreams. You've got to be hard-headed in this business."

For some reason, it made LD feel embarrassed — embarrassed and foolishly happy.

CHAPTER 19

"Then, after the raid," Wheels intoned, "I'm gonna get me a new jacket and put the Cannibals' crest right in the middle of it. And everyone on the street will know I'm somebody!"

"Yick!" Susie hissed. "That's the cue for the ghost. Where is it?"

"It's coming," Yick said, and he turned the handle to send the glowing apparition onstage. Slowly it glided from the wings, stage left, a vague luminous shape in shades of purple and ghastly green, bobbing and floating in the darkness. The handful of people watching the dress rehearsal burst into applause.

"Very effective," Ms. Avery said. "It's going to look great." At the beginning of the dress rehearsal, she had told everyone they should think of this as a real performance, but almost nothing had gone the way it should, and they had stopped frequently. There had been Snake's difficulty hearing the actors from the lighting booth, for example, which sometimes plunged a scene into total darkness. There was Lucky's inability to find his baseball bat — a crucial prop in Act Three, Scene Five. Then there had been several occasions when LD and the set changers ("Great name for a band," Snake quipped) had presented the wrong segment of the turntable. Yick's small delay in producing the ghost seemed almost trivial.

Backstage, Susie slipped a cough drop in her mouth, and called across the stage, "It's perfect, Yick. Just be sure to make your cue." She looked again at the ghost. The ultraviolet light must be playing tricks on her. It looked like there was a cloud of mist around the phantom. Mist . . . or smoke.

"What's that smell?" Ms. Avery said.

Susie sniffed and shrugged. "I can't smell anything anyway."

"Maybe it's the plastic of the raincoat," Ms. Avery said. "Let's go on."

"Right. Wheels, can you go on from there, please?"

"And, Yick," Ms. Avery called, "keep the ghost swaying. It has to move all the time." Obediently Yick began to tug at the line, which would ultimately turn the ghost back to front, in order to display the hideous red gash in its back. In response, the ghost swooped and bounded like a kite. "Wonderful!" Ms. Avery said. "Eddy?"

Wheels had been standing patiently in the middle of the roof set. Now he turned toward the ghost and resumed his character. "Who's that?" he said in apparent alarm. The phantom advanced menacingly toward him. From the speakers flanking the stage came the groan of Wheels' own bass, being tortured unmusically by Snake. "Who's there? Get away from me, I tell you! Get away!!"

The groaning was joined by an unearthly screech from Snake's guitar, as the ghost made a sudden lurch toward Wheels.

At that moment, to his astonishment, Wheels saw a thread of real fire kindle in the heart of the apparition. Sparks began to pour out of it, cascading onto the stage.

Wheels forgot about being Eddy. "What the —" he began, and then the ghost lurched at him again. It suddenly seemed to have a life of its own. "Get out of here!" he blurted, and kicked into the folds of plastic. Something snakelike, hissing fire at one end, fell out of the raincoat. Then, while Snake's unholy din continued to pour from the speakers, Yick's firecrackers began to explode.

"Yeow!!!" Wheels leaped backward, tripped on the edge of the platform, and did a backward roll past Susie into the wings. Pungent smoke filled the stage, and for a few seconds Snake's ghost sounds were drowned out in the rapid-fire gunshots of the writhing string of fireworks.

When at last the noise died away, there was silence. Ms. Avery had been watching open-mouthed. Now she stood up. "Everyone else take a break," she said evenly. "Yick! We need to talk . . . "

Yick's face was the picture of unhappiness. "They weren't actually supposed to explode," he said. He and Ms. Avery were sitting in the green room. She had sent everyone else away.

"But what were they doing there in the first place?" she demanded. "*Why* would you put firecrackers inside the ghost?"

Yick felt a drop of sweat run down his back "Sort of a custom?" he offered. "Chinese custom?" It wasn't really a custom. The whole thing was Yick's idea of what might work to keep the spook harmless. The fact that it had gone wrong only confirmed his idea that the supernatural was not to be trusted.

To Yick's relief, Ms. Avery didn't ask about the custom. She looked at him a moment. "Then, how did the fuse get lit?"

"Uh . . . well, there was a little stick of incense, see . . . and, uh, it must have moved . . . "

"When the ghost was bouncing around," she concluded. "Yick, do you know how lucky we were? There could have been a fire. Wheels could have been seriously hurt. At the very least, your ghost could have blown up. Anything could have happened. We're very, very lucky to get away with just scorched paint. I accept that you did this for your own good reason, but I need to know if you can promise me it won't happen again. Because if you can't, I'll have to get someone else to run the ghost. That's all there is to it."

Something Ms. Avery said clicked inside Yick's head, and to her surprise, he grinned. "Sure," he said. "I promise."

"No more firecrackers? No more incense? No more *anything* unless you tell me first?"

"I promise," he repeated. "No more surprises."

She looked at him doubtfully and then said, "Okay. Then, let's go. This run-through is taking a long time . . . "

Yick followed her out of the green room with a lightness he had not felt for weeks. Really, he thought, he should have seen it sooner. The incense and firecrackers *had* worked. They had been lucky! If evil spirits had been at work, probably the whole school would be just a smoking crater right now. But it wasn't! Now the show could go on — in safety.

The dress rehearsal dragged slowly

onward as the cast and crew went through their paces. LD sat backstage, waiting for the moments when she and her band of trusty scenery changes were to scuttle forward and transform segments of the turntable — which now, mercifully, worked. Like the other set changers, she was wearing black: black top, black tights and black cloth shoes. That way, if they were glimpsed through a gap in the curtains, they would not distract from the action. LD was also wearing a black sweater, because it was cool and drafty backstage and she was afraid of catching Susie's cold. The actors were even more fearful of such a possibility. Everyone made large detours whenever they encountered the suffering stage manager.

Finally, after everyone had been bored cross-eyed, the last curtain came down. Ms. Avery called them all together onstage.

"Believe it or not, we're looking good," she said. "Not perfect, but good. If we can just fix up the things I told you about, and, ahem, avoid any surprises — " She looked pointedly at Yick, " — we should be all right tomorrow. Theater people believe that if you have a bad dress rehearsal, you'll have a good opening. That's why they say, 'Break a leg.' So, according to that theory, we should be in great shape. Cast and make-up people, be here at six tomorrow. Crew be here at six-thirty. Front of house, be here at a quarter past seven. I'm looking forward to it." She looked around at them and smiled tiredly. "And now," she said, "I suggest you all go out, have a pizza, and forget about the play for tonight!"

CHAPTER 20

They hit the pizza shop like an avalanche and filled every booth. "I can't believe it," Lucy said, throwing herself back against the red leatherette. "I didn't think we were ever going to finish that rehearsal!"

"Same here!" Wheels said, sitting down beside her.

"*I* didn't believe we were ever going to *get* to that rehearsal!" LD replied from across the table. "A week ago, we had some unpainted flats and a mattress. Now we've got *sets*!"

Joey was in the booth behind LD. At her declaration, his head snapped around. "Now you've got *what*?" he demanded. "Want to share? Joey S-F Jeremiah, at your service. S-F for sex fiend, of course."

"Sets, Joey, sets!" Lucy said. "As in scenery?"

"Oh. Sure," said Joey. "I like scenery, too. Of the female kind!"

LD looked at Joey and said with a straight face, "Better not hang around backstage, Joey. You might get caught in a set change operation."

Lucy groaned and rolled her eyes. Just then Snake slid in beside LD and said, "Are you going to trade in your hard hat for a fireman's helmet?"

LD hooted. "Those firecrackers! Poor Wheels, you must have thought you were under attack!"

"I thought I was going crazy!" Wheels said. "Or maybe something weird was going on with the black light."

"With my lights?" Snake demanded in mock outrage. "How can you even suggest such a thing? LD, did you talk to Yick about it!"

"Oh, yeah," LD said. "As soon as Ms. Avery was through with him. I threatened to put his head in a vice unless he promised the ghost would run without gunpowder. I don't know why he did it."

"He told me it was an accident," Snake said. "I'd hate to see what he could do on purpose!"

It was late when they finally left the pizza shop and headed in their separate directions.

It had also turned wet, and cold. The black pavement gleamed slickly in the street lights. Lucy, Wheels, Snake and LD walked together, still too wide awake to want to go home.

"I wonder how long it's been raining," LD said.

"More than rain," Lucy said, peering up into the sky. "Look. That's snow."

It was true. Thick wet flakes of spring snow had begun to tumble out of the sky. Faster and faster it came, until in a moment they were all cloaked in white.

"You've got white hair," LD said to Snake. "They're even on your eyelashes."

Snake fluttered his eyes. "Not on yours, though," he said, and flicked the bill of her cap. A miniature snowfall tumbled into her face.

"Hey! Phh! It's even in my nose," she said.

Snake bent over and shook his head like a shaggy dog, so that more snow sprayed in her face. "Don't!" she laughed. She pulled off her cap and tried to hit him with it, but he dodged away. Then she shook her head, and turned her face up to the falling snow. "I can feel it on my eyelids."

Snake stopped and turned his face up as well. For a moment they stood motionless, feeling the snowflakes land on their faces. Then Snake said, "I 'an 'eel 'em on my 'ongue."

LD began to laugh. She stuck out her tongue, too, and said, "Wunh, wunh 'oo, wunh 'oo 'hwhee . . . " The two of them were suddenly hooting uproariously, wandering along on the sidewalk with their tongues out, talking, laughing and trying to catch snowflakes all at the same time. Then, when it seemed the laughter was dying away, they looked ahead and saw Wheels and Lucy staring incredulously back at them. Instantly they fell into fresh convulsions, and when those began to fade, Snake barely saved himself from walking into a lamp-post and they had to laugh about that, too. At last, when all the laughter had been shaken out of them, they found that Wheels and Lucy had gone on ahead. They were alone on the street.

"Come on," Snake said. "I'll walk you home."

"Okay."

"Can I wear your hat?"

"What for? Are you cold?"

"No. I just want to."

"Sure, I guess so." She gave it to him, but instead of putting it on the right way, he put it on back to front. "There," he said, "ready to cue the lights." And he pointed at a burnt-out streetlight.

"Nothing happened," LD said.

Snake shrugged. "It's probably wired

through Yick's effects panel."

They walked on in silence for a ways, and then LD said, "Snake? Tell me something. How come you didn't take off like everyone else when I was being so awful?"

The snowstorm was ending as quickly as it had come. A few last flakes drifted down. Snake kicked at a rapidly dissolving footprint. "Oh ... I dunno. Practice, I guess."

"Practice?"

"Yeah. My mom ... sometimes she has moods. She doesn't mean anything by it. But you have to keep your head down."

"Moods?"

He was silent for a moment. Then he said, "Sometimes she gets sort of violent. Yells. Maybe throws things. She takes pills for it," he added. "Most of the time she's okay — but you never know. That's why I never ask anyone over ... I've never told anyone about it before, either."

It was LD's turn to be silent. "I won't tell anyone," she said at last. "But you didn't have to stay around the shop, like you do at home. Why didn't you just leave?"

They were almost at Lucy's house. Snake grinned at her and said, "Just dumb, I guess. Dumb enough to think you're neat." Then he shoved the cap back on her head, pulled the bill low over her face, and said, "See you tomorrow, LD. Break a leg!"

"Yeah," LD said with a foolish grin. "Break two." And then she turned, sprinted up the walk, and took the front steps in one leap.

CHAPTER 21

The next morning LD showed up at the school in a kind of euphoric haze. She had dreamed of walking with someone through a curtain of snowflakes magically lit by streetlights, and echoes of the dream still lingered with her. Almost as good, her work on the play was done. She would help change sets, of course, but only as cued by Susie. Compared to the breakneck pace of the last two months, that was nothing. And between set changes, she had decided, she would sit in the lighting booth with Snake, and watch the play from there.

The first person she saw backstage was Ms. Avery. "Hi, Ms. Avery," she said. "Tonight's the night!"

"LD," Ms. Avery said. "I've been looking

for you. You're going to have to be in charge back here tonight."

LD laughed. "I thought you were in charge, Ms. Avery."

"That's not what I mean, LD. Susie's sick. She's got laryngitis and can't speak above a whisper. You've got to fill in for her."

"But . . . I can't!" LD said. "What about Snake? Or Shane?"

"Snake can't leave the booth. I trust you."

"But I don't know the cues!" LD protested. "How *can* I do it?"

"I've got Susie's book," Ms. Avery said. "She's got cues written in, if you can read them. So, sit down here at the prompter's table, and take a look at it. Then make sure everyone is on their mark at eight. You can take the curtain up two minutes late, in case of latecomers. Have you got a watch?"

"Uh . . . yeah . . . "

"Good. I'll be around until the house opens, in case you want to ask me anything. Now sit down and look over Susie's script."

Dismayed, LD slid into Susie's chair and flipped open her copy of the play. At the bottom of the first page was a scribbled note outlined in heavy red marker: *Blurk thog gm tibble Eddy.* LD held her head in her hands. Why, oh, why did Susie have to make her notes in a foreign language?'

At five minutes to eight, LD peeked

through the curtain at the audience. The auditorium was almost full. Ms. Avery and Mr. Raditch were in the front row. Two rows behind them, she could see both of Lucy's parents. She had a momentary pang of regret that her father could not be there. But on the other hand, she thought, if it turned out to be a disaster, it could be a good thing he wasn't there.

She turned from the curtain and walked across the sweep of the turntable toward the green room. As she went, she passed Joey, Alex and Wheels standing in the wings, and mentally checked them off. "All set?" she said.

"You bet," Joey said.

"Great. Break a leg!"

She got to the green room, stuck her head inside and saw Lucy, Steph and Erica perched on the edges of their chairs. Most of the rest of the cast was there, some talking nervously, others too nervous to talk at all. LD scanned them, counting on her fingers. Finally she said, "Where's Arthur?"

"The last I saw him, he was getting his make-up put on," Steph said.

"He should be here already." LD started to go to the dressing rooms, but then looked at her watch. There was no time. She turned back to the stage, spotted Yick and grabbed him. "Does the ghost work?" she demanded.

Yick nodded vigorously. "Sure, LD."

"Good. Go down the boys' dressing room

and get Arthur up to the green room. We start in two minutes, and I want him ready!"

Yick saluted and disappeared. LD turned and peered up into the lighting cage suspended a dozen feet up in the wings. By the dim glow of panel lights, she made out Snake sitting on a stool. Behind him were propped the guitar and bass. "Are you ready?" she hissed.

"Can't get any readier," he called down in a low voice. "Break an arm!"

"Yeah, right. Or a neck." She went to her chair, sat down, and put on the headset that connected her to Snake, Yick and Kathleen, who was in charge of front of house. She pointed to Joey, Alex and Wheels, who walked on stage and took their places. Then she spoke into the mike. "Ready, front of house?"

"Hi, LD. Last ones just going in."

"Ready, special effects?"

There was a scrambling sound, and Yick said breathlessly, "LD? Arthur just came up."

"Great," LD said. "Thank you. Are *you* ready?"

"Yes, ready."

"Ready, lights?"

"Yup. Still ready."

LD looked at her watch and took a deep breath. "Okay. Cue the stage . . . " Rows of floodlights came on overhead, bathing the waiting actors in a blue-white radiance. " . . . house lights down . . . and . . . curtain! . . . "

The play had begun.

If she had had the time, LD might have wondered why the play went by so quickly, when the dress rehearsal had taken forever. But she was too busy. She had her first moment of panic when Arthur missed his cue. Stephanie delivered the line that was to bring him on stage and looked expectantly into the wings, but her son Chip did not appear. LD felt her heart stop. Valiantly treading water, Steph made up a short speech about how her son was always late. "Never on time," she chattered, "always up to something," while LD sprinted to the green room, grabbed Arthur by the collar and practically threw him onstage. "Oh, there you are, Chip," Steph cooed as he stumbled into view. "Mind your step, dear. I've been looking for you . . . " And she gave him his cue again.

After that, LD was expecting trouble, but it didn't come for a while. She had her moments of anxiety around Yick's effects, but the sirens and flashing lights worked when they were supposed to. In fact, they all got to the end of the third act without further mishap.

As the curtain came down for the intermission, LD got up to walk around the turntable and check out her scenery shifters —

and narrowly escaped a collision with a bat-swinging Joey, still wild from his exit as the hard-hitting leader of the Cannibals.

LD ducked. "Whoa! Joey! Take it easy!"

Joey made a tough-guy face and held the end of the bat in front of her face. "This is Cannibal turf, see?"

"Yeah, right. Just don't swing that bat back here." She went on making her rounds, checking on everyone, including the set changers, who had to work without her tonight.

"No sweat," Shane told her. "We got it covered, LD."

Her last stop was to climb the rungs to the lighting cage. "Hi," she said. "How's it going?"

"Piece of cake," Snake said. "Can't wait to play my ghost music. Do you think I could play a little warm-up during the intermission?"

"Oh, sure," LD said offhandedly. "Might as well." Snake reached for the guitar and she grabbed his wrist. "Don't you dare!" she said.

Snake grinned. "You're probably right. Better to surprise them."

LD grinned, too, then looked at her watch. "Ready to go in two?"

"Two for you," he said. "Too-ti-too-too-too."

"You're hilarious," she said drily. "I think the electrons up here have erased your brain.

You can start dimming the house lights — "
She checked her watch again. " — now." And
she climbed down out of the cage.

But as she was making her way to the
prompter's table, she suddenly tripped and
fell sprawling forward on her face.

"LD? Are you all right?" It was Lucy,
standing ready for her entrance at the beginning of the next act.

"I think so," LD said. "I tripped on something." She groped in the shadows around
her feet and found a handful of tangled nylon
fishing line. In the middle dangled a small
brass pulley. She stared at it stupidly for a
second, and then reality flashed on her like
a strobe light. It was Yick's ghost track.
Joey must have swiped it accidentally with
his bat as he made his exit.

And the ghost was due on in about five
minutes . . .

Just then she heard Snake warning her
from above. "House lights are down, LD,"
he said. "Ready to roll . . . "

What on earth could she do? "Uh . . .
places," she hissed, "and curtain . . . !"

CHAPTER 22

Carmen took a step toward Eddy. "I heard the Cannibals are planning a raid, Eddy."

"So?"

"So what are you going to do?"

"What's that to you?"

"Eddy," she said, "there's no need for this fight! The Cannibals and the Scorpions always got along before. It's just Lucky! He's trying to stir something up, don't you see?"

"The Scorpions knocked off Sharkey."

"Who says so?"

"Lucky says so. He was there. He saw it."

"Then how come Sharkey was stabbed in the back?"

"What? How do you know that? You never saw him."

"I know, Eddy. Believe me!"

"Ah, you're making it up!"

"I'm not! I seen — "

"What?"

"I . . . once, in the moonlight . . . I saw his ghost . . . "

"His ghost? Aw, you're crazy! Get out of here!"

"But, Eddy — "

"I mean it, Carmen! Get out of here! I got some thinking to do, and I don't need you to help me."

Carmen stood in silence for a moment, and then said, "Have it your way, Eddy. But you'll see. I'm right. I'm right!!" Then she whirled and dashed offstage.

Eddy looked after her for a second, and then began to pace around the roof, deep in thought. "Aw, what does she know?" he said. "Ghosts! Ghosts don't even exist! They don't mean nothing. What means something is to be somebody when you're alive. And I'm going to be a Cannibal, just as soon as this raid is over. Just a little Scorpion blood on my knife — " He pulled out the slim blade and held it so the light ran along it. " — and I'm in. After the raid, I'm gonna get me a new jacket and put the Cannibals' crest right in the middle of it. And everyone on the street will know I'm somebody!" Eddy now turned toward stage left, anticipating the ghost to come swaying out of the darkness toward him.

Inside Eddy, Wheels braced himself, wondering if the ghost would behave this time.

He heard the first amplified groans from the speakers, but there was no sign of the apparition. As casually as he could, Wheels peered into the shadows, trying to conjure a ghost out of the patches of light that now began to dance before his straining eyes. He was about to repeat his cue, when the ghost suddenly materialized right beside him.

Whatever it was, it wasn't Yick's raincoat hanging from some fishing line! A crouching, glowing something lurched from side to side, bobbing and weaving in a place quite different from where the raincoat should have been. And — worse — there was no made-up balloon head, but the fright wig floated in the air anyway. Then the guitar shrieked. Or was it the guitar? Wheels, unnerved, wasn't sure.

"Who's ... who's there?" he shouted hoarsely. "Who is it? Get away from me!" It was Wheels' most convincing performance yet.

"Sharkey? Is that you?"

The phantom flapped its arms and made a sudden flying hop onto the turntable, almost landing on Wheels. But Wheels was making his own hop backward — a clear six feet, and he was ready for more if the ghost advanced any further. "Sharkey," he said with a voice that barely shook, "take it easy, Sharkey. Me and the Cannibals been thinking about you. We got a surprise coming for the Scorpions. You'd like that, wouldn't ya?"

Ghastly sounds crawled out of the speakers, and the ghost twisted and thrashed in denial like a soul in torment.

"But . . . the Scorpions did you in, didn't they?"

More thrashing, more horrible sounds.

"Luce . . . I mean, Carmen said Lucky killed you. Stabbed you in the back. It isn't true, is it?"

The wailing and gnashing of strings reached a crescendo, and with a massive effort, the ghost leaped into the air and spun around, to show the lurid, nine-inch wound glowing a brilliant scarlet under the ultraviolet light. For a moment it hung poised in mid-air, arms spread, while Eddy absorbed this. Then it disappeared, stage left, as suddenly as a blown-out candle flame.

When Wheels was able to make his own exit, the first person he found in the wings was Yick.

"What *was* that?" Wheels demanded.

"It was . . . um . . . uh — " Yick gestured and Wheels turned to find the ghost standing beside him. Before his astonished eyes, the arms of the raincoat suddenly produced hands, then reached up and moved the wig. By some magic a face appeared above its shoulders. It was LD's face, and it was laughing.

"You should have seen yourself," she sputtered in a half-choked whisper. " 'Who's there? Get away from me!' . . . You were

177

great, Wheels! Exit ghost, stage left!"

And she disappeared again in the dark.

When the play was over and the cast took its curtain calls, bouquets of flowers appeared from nowhere. Wheels came out with a bunch of pink roses for Lucy, and then Lucy and Erica produced a large bunch of red roses for Ms. Avery, who came and joined them on the stage. Then, while the applause continued to rain down, Ms. Avery said something to Joey, who ran off and returned with LD, still wearing most of the ghost costume. She felt a little dumb, taking a bow with the cast, but at least the applause drowned out the rustling of the plastic raincoat.

Later, when she and Snake locked up and walked home, he said, "Pretty good debut, LD. I didn't know you could act."

"Are you kidding? I can't," LD said.

"But those moves, LD. You were fantastic! Wildly out of control, if you know what I mean. You had me spooked! I thought, whoa, what if she tries to get up into the booth?"

LD laughed. "Sure, I was spooked myself. I was caught in Yick's fishing line, that's all. It was dark back there, and by the time I had the sweater pulled up over my head, I couldn't see a thing. Maybe if I hadn't been so wired about getting out there, I would have felt it, but I didn't. Then, when I went through the curtain, it just pulled tight around my ankles like a noose. Every time I moved, I thought, this is it, I'm going to fall on my face."

Snake laughed. "You could have really broken a leg for us!"

"Yeah. Or my nose. You think that's funny?"

Snake was instantly serious. "Certainly not," he said, "and I think the Student Council ought to pass a bylaw against it, just to keep it that way." Then he started to laugh again. "But Wheels was pretty funny ... "

"You should have seen his face when I hopped up on the turntable! I thought, if he kicks the ghost like he did at dress rehearsal, I'm dead!"

"So, are you going to put the pulleys back up for tomorrow night?"

LD stopped laughing long enough to consider this. "No ... I don't think so. Wheels might be disappointed if the ghost came out normally. But I definitely will sweep the stage before the curtain goes up!"

Much later, after a satisfying good-night to Snake, LD sat down at the kitchen table with a piece of paper. She didn't want to sleep yet, and she thought maybe she should write a letter to her dad. She wondered if

179

there was time for it to get to him in Corsica. Probably not. Oh, well, she could just leave it at the garage for him . . .

She stared into space for a long time, thinking about all the things that had happened on the way to opening night and then about the play. How could she put all that in a letter? Finally, she picked up her pen and wrote: "Dear Dad, Having a wonderful time, wish you were here. Come back soon. Love, Lorraine."

CHAPTER 23

It was a huge cast party. Mr. Raditch had suggested they use the school auditorium, since most of the school had worked on the play, but Lucy had offered her house, and that was the popular choice. People were crammed in every corner, talking nose to nose above the frantic beat of the stereo. Lucy's mother had stayed long enough to uncrate a carload of pop and snack food, and then she had prudently left. Ms. Avery and Mr. Raditch stayed a little longer, mingling with their colleagues of the theater.

"Hi, LD." A slow-moving eddy through the solidly packed living room brought Ms. Avery face to face with her master carpenter. "Loud, isn't it?"

"Sure is!" LD had to shout to be heard.

Beside them, in an open space no bigger than a telephone booth, Wheels and Lucy were trying to dance.

Ms. Avery hoisted her glass out of the way of a sudden jostle, and then leaned toward LD. "I wanted to tell you, LD, that I thought you did an excellent job."

"Thanks, Ms. Avery. On the sets, you mean?"

"Yes, on the sets. That turntable was very professional-looking. And as a ghost."

LD laughed. She had already told Ms. Avery about the fishing line. "I guess I just got wrapped up in my work," she said.

Ms. Avery laughed. "It's just too bad your father wasn't here to see it. Ask him to give me a call when he gets back, and I'll tell him all about it."

"Okay, I will. Thanks, Ms. Avery."

In the kitchen, where the light was brighter and the music slightly dimmer, Arthur and Yick stood wedged with Melanie between the table and an angle of the counter. Yick was wearing an orange plastic headband from which sprouted long, antenna-like springs. On the ends of the springs bobbed red hearts. Someone had written on the headband, "Kiss me, I'm a Cannibal!" There was a small dagger sticking into one of the hearts.

"Uh . . . very nice," Arthur said, looking

at the headband. "Very unusual. Where did you get it?"

"I found it in my locker," Yick said.

Arthur looked at Melanie. "Did you know that Yick's locker is the exit of a mysterious time-warp?"

"Actually," said Yick, "it's all because of friendly spirits. Next, I'm hoping they'll do my homework for me."

"Spirits?" Melanie said. "*You* are in contact with spirits? How interesting!" Just then they were pressed against the table by a slow collision of people looking for the lemonade and others heading toward the music.

"You know," Melanie said, "I think there would be more room *under* the table."

"Sure," Yick said. "Good idea." Carefully he folded himself under the chip dip. Melanie followed him, but when Arthur prepared to do the same, he found there was no more room.

"Sorry," Melanie said. "Could you pass us the potato chips? Thanks. Now, what about these spirits . . . ?"

Since the cast party was for everybody, there were no "official" dates, but Stephanie had brought one anyway. After the last curtain call of the last performance, when everyone backstage was bouncing off the walls with the hysteria of having made it, she went up to Joey. "Hi! You going to the cast party?"

Joey was still in "Lucky" mode. "Hey, baby — I *am* the party."

"Cause if you are," Steph said, "I wondered if you'd go with me."

Suddenly Joey was himself, looking at her warily. "Just as a friend," Steph added hastily. "No tricks this time. You can say no if you want to. But I'd like to be friends with you, Joey. What do you say?"

He hesitated an instant longer, and then his face split open in a wide grin. His teeth were bright against the darkness of his make-up. "You got a date, Mrs. Wark," he said. "I always liked ya better than your daughter anyway!"

All of which explained why, when the party had thinned out a little, and the dance space grew to a phone-booth-and-a-half, Stephanie and Joey were sharing the floor with Lucy and Wheels. Trying to dance at such close quarters was a little like four people taking a shower together, except that they were being sprayed with music instead of water.

When one tape ran out, Lucy stretched around Erica, Heather and Voula to find another. "I've got a great album here by Left Tibia," she said. "Somewhere."

Caitlyn, who had been standing on the

perimeter watching them dance, said, "Gee, Wheels, it's too bad your band couldn't play for the party."

Wheels glanced involuntarily at Joey. "Ah, yeah, well, you know how it is . . . sort of crowded, anyway."

But Stephanie wouldn't let it pass. "Listen, Wheels," she said, "I have to tell you something." Just then the metal sounds of Left Tibia began to boom and vibrate through the house, and Steph grabbed Wheels and pulled him into a corner. Joey looked at Lucy, shrugged, and began to dance with her. Taking advantage of the extra space, Erica began to dance with Voula.

Wheels and Stephanie stayed huddled in the corner for a long time. From time to time he would glance over his shoulder at Joey and then shout a question at her. Then he would listen some more.

At last, Left Tibia shuddered to a halt. "Hoo, I need some air," Lucy said.

Steph, abandoning Wheels, said, "Me, too. I'll come with you."

The two slipped away through the crowd, and Joey suddenly found himself standing beside Wheels. He was about to turn away when Wheels said, "Wait a minute, Joey. I owe you an apology. Steph just pointed out I've been a total jerk and a bag-head. I think I let this play get in the way of everything, including my brain." He paused. "I'm sorry."

There was an awkward moment. Then Joey grinned. "Hey, Wheels, my man, no problem!" And somehow they found room for their private hi-jive handshake. "When's our next band practice?"

"When we wake up, I guess," Wheels replied, "in about six weeks!"

Lucy and Steph didn't venture far outside for their breath of air. If they had, they might have spotted two dark shapes sitting close together on the garden swing in the backyard. The shapes belonged to Snake and LD.

"Are you warm enough?" Snake asked after they had watched Steph and Lucy go back inside.

"I'm all right," LD said. It had warmed up a little, and the night air had the first cool scents of spring on it — thawing earth and old, wet grass. Unable to talk inside, the two had put on coats and slipped outside. Now, though, they sat in silence.

The swing swayed gently. In front of them, they could see a rectangle of star-lit sky, fringed with the bare branches of maples. Down in one corner hung the silver sickle of a new moon. From time to time they heard the noise of the party get louder as someone opened the front door to go home. Then it would subside again, and they would be left in their private bubble of silence.

At last, after a long time, the lights of an airplane tracked across the sky just where they were watching.

Gently, Snake squeezed LD's hand. "Shooting star. Make a wish."

She looked at him and started to speak. Then she thought better of it and made a wish. But neither of them said what they wished for. After another long silence, when the moon had finally slipped from view, LD said, "Exit moon, stage left."

Snake looked at her in mock alarm. "Is it curtains for us?"

She grinned. "I don't think so. It's still the first act, isn't it?"

He gave her hand another squeeze and said, "You bet. Act One, Scene One . . . Ghost and electrician by moonlight — uh, make that starlight . . . Noises are heard off . . . " As if on cue, the sounds of the party swelled momentarily, and the night was briefly stitched with someone's laughter.

LD knew that in a while she would go inside, and make her way through the remains of the party to bed, where she would fall asleep instantly. She was very tired. But she was also very happy, and for just a little while longer, she didn't want to change a thing.

WILLIAM PASNAK is a freelance writer living in Calgary, Alberta. His first novel for children, *In the City of the King* (Groundwood, 1984) received the W. Ross Annett award from the Writers Guild of Alberta. A sequel, *Under the Eagle's Claw*, will be released in the Spring of 1988. He is presently at work on another children's novel, *Matthew's Summer*, and a non-fiction book about Alberta. When he is not writing books, he writes magazine articles and scripts for educational TV.